THE HIRELING

A NOVELLA OF ADVENTURE FANTASY

STEFON MEARS

Thousand
Faces
Publishing

Also by Stefon Mears

The Rise of Magic Series
Magician's Choice
Sleight of Mind
Lunar Alchemy
Three Fae Monte
The Sphinx Principle
Double Backed Magic
Mercury Fold (forthcoming)

Cavan Oltblood Series
Half a Wizard
The Ice Dagger
Spells of Undeath

Power City Tales
Not Quite Bulletproof
No Money in Heroism

Standalones
The Hireling
The Captain's Cat
Save Whiskers!
The Ogre of Threepeaks
Between the Cracks
Sects and the City
Prince of a Thousand Worlds
Devil's Night
Portal-Land, Oregon
Stealing from Pirates
Fade to Gold
With a Broken Sword
Twice Against the Dragon
The House on Cedar Street
Sudden Death
On the Edge of Faerie

Short Story Collections
Spell Slingers
Twisted Timelines
Longhairs and Short Tales: A Collection of Cat Stories
Dangerous Space
Confronting Legends (Spells & Swords Vol. 1)
The Patreon Collection, Vol. 1-8 (Vol. 9, coming soon)

Nonfiction
The 30-Day Novel and Beyond!

Spells for Hire Series
Devil's Shoestring
Zombie Powder
Spirit Trap
Dragon's Blood

The Telepath Trilogy
Surviving Telepathy
Immoral Telepathy
Targeting Telepathy

Edge of Humanity Series
Caught Between Monsters
Hunting Monsters

Jumpstart Duchy Series
Into the Torn Kingdoms
The Dragon's Gold
The Gift Castle
The Deadly Feast
The King's Test
Triumph in the Torn Kingdoms

Published by Thousand Faces Publishing, Portland, Oregon

http://1kfaces.com

Front cover image © Sasinparaksa | Dreamstime.com (File ID: 118204528)

ISBN: 978-1-948490-52-8

THE HIRELING

My friends all said I was crazy, trying to get a job at the Purple Gryphon. But let's be honest here. The Purple Gryphon *was* Terand's Bend.

Yes, Terand's Bend had existed as a township for maybe two hundred years before Kue Rinton opened the Purple Gryphon, back when my folks were just taking over grampa's farm and I was maybe a year or two away from being born.

But it was the Purple Gryphon that made the mapmakers take notice of us. The Purple Gryphon that brought in the business that built our inns and put coins in the pockets of our smiths and crafters and merchants. And made Market Day a whole lot busier.

Dyaphane's Blood, the business from the Purple Gryphon enabled my parents to *double* their number of farmhands and expand their sweet beans and taro grains into *twelve full fields*.

Had I been the oldest, I'd've been happy to work that farm my whole life, and live pretty comfortably, thanks to the Purple Gryphon.

But Miphon was older than me by four years, and he and I got along about as well as sweet beans and rocksoil. The last thing I wanted was to live under his thumb once my parents died.

So by the time I reached the age where some of my friends – the ones who weren't staying with *their* family farms – were fighting over apprenticeships, I knew I wanted something else out of life.

I wanted to go where the action was.

I wanted to work at the Purple Gryphon.

So on the morning after Market Day, I was up before dawn. Washed myself good, downed a portion of porridge with extra chicken, and dressed in my best pale brown tunic over dark brown breeches, with soft shoes of dark gray.

I was particularly proud of the shoes. First ones I'd owned with leather soles.

I'd gotten the leather from Yinda's family, when I'd helped them catch and put down a cow that'd run amuck.

The meat was no good. Whatever weed the poor thing had gotten into had soured it. But the hide was fine, and for my help I'd been awarded a square as long as my forearm. Enough for not only soles for my new shoes, but a pair of gloves as well. And I wore those gloves on my belt when I dressed that day, to show that I had them ready if I needed them.

Not that I expected to. The thaws had finished and we were fully into spring now. With the morning air full of the smell of budding orange blossoms – a good sign for the orange crops this year – and sweet scents from the river, which was running high from all the meltwater coming down from the mountains to the north.

Yinda met up with me as I left the farm that morning, just as the sky was starting to gray with the coming dawn. Yinda was my age, or close enough to it, but she was two full heads shorter than me, and so frail a stiff wind might whisk her away to get caught in tree branches.

Legacy of an old illness, that frailty. She'd spent a whole summer and part of an autumn sick in bed, gasping for every wet breath before finally fighting it off with the help of poultices from that wise woman who'd come up from Falling Rock.

But I'll tell you. What Yinda lacked in size and muscle, she made up in pure willpower. Even a mule knew better than to try to out-stubborn Yinda.

Not quite true to say she fell into step beside me, when she joined me. Too short for that. But she'd long ago made clear that I was not to shorten my stride for her. Instead she'd trained herself to keep up.

"You going to see Mattias?" I asked. She certainly had the fingers to make a good tailor. Slender and clever.

Yinda scoffed. "Try Bolan."

I stopped suddenly enough to kick up a small dust cloud. Yinda, however, kept walking. Not that I needed long to catch up.

"You been eating from that cow's trough?" I asked. "Gotta have muscle to be a blacksmith."

"Muscle will come," she said. "And you're the crazy one, Zian Sonnalsson. People get *murdered* at the Purple Gryphon."

"They do *not*."

"They *do*. They just dispose of the bodies real quiet like, so as not to upset the customers."

"Turn the corpses into stew, do they?"

"Don't be stupid. That Kue Rinton's a witch. Everyone knows it. So she just charms away the mess and has the bodies snuck out under cover of night." Yinda gave me a firm nod. "Happens once a week, at the least."

"Oh, really?"

"Yes, really. And if you'd ever clean the dirt out of your ears, I wouldn't have to be the one telling you."

Oh, that was one of Yinda's favorite things to say to me. She'd been saying it as long as I could remember. Even though I'd years ago learned to clean my ears properly.

"And just how did *you* hear about it, if it's such a secret?"

"Tonny's cousins, Uli and Juli. They snuck into the stables one night to look at the horses. You know they always have the best horses."

That much was true. Travelers came from far and wide to visit the Purple Gryphon, and many of them were so rich they could spend the kind of money on a horse that most of us would spend on a year's trade goods.

"And just what did those two worthies see, from their hiding place?"

"Purple-eyed Kue Rinton herself, directing two of her lackies who were carrying something big, bulky and wrapped in roughspun. Snuck it out in the dead of night, they did."

"Well, just call the watch and send for the justiciar," I said, voice dripping with sarcasm. "If that's not hard proof of murder, I don't know what is."

"Walk around with both eyes closed like that, Zian Sonnalsson, and you'll walk right into walls."

Her tone was so affronted that I sighed.

"Well if they're only killing travelers, I should be just fine."

Yinda stopped and grabbed me by the hand.

"You watch yourself, Zian," she said, voice low and sincere. "That Kue Rinton's a witch, or I didn't spend a whole summer fighting for air."

Funny thing was, Yinda and I were at an age then that if any other girl grabbed me by the hand that way, my breath would've caught and I'd've felt hot all over.

But Yinda, she was more like my sister than a real girl, you know? And I know she didn't see me as a boy, either, so much as a brother who didn't happen to share her parents.

So when it was Yinda grabbing my hand that way, I knew it was just worry and nothing else.

"I'll be all right," I said. "And I'll keep both eyes and ears open. I promise."

"You see that you do." She narrowed her eyes at me. "Because I'll kill that witch myself if anything happens to you." She jabbed me in the chest with a finger. "And if I do that, I'll *never* get to be a smith, now will I?"

Oh, and I did the worst thing I possibly could have.

I chuckled.

She jabbed my chest with her finger again.

"Think it's funny, do you?" She shook her head. "Well, we'll just see who's laughing, won't we?"

She turned and stomped off. And for someone so small, she did an admirable job of impersonating and angry bull.

And me, I headed off for the Purple Gryphon.

***

Despite the impression I might've given Yinda, she wasn't the first person I'd heard say that people got murdered at the Purple Gryphon. But the thing was, there were so many stories about the place, who could possibly believe them all?

And if you can't believe them all, how can you pick and choose which ones *to* believe?

Just to give you an idea, I'd heard...

...that all the major thieves guilds sent representatives to the Purple Gryphon at least twice each season to make deals and move major stolen goods.

...that half of the clientele were those so-called adventurers. The type who were said to delve into ancient crypts and ruins, looking for lost treasures of one kind or another.

...that a cabal of wizards met there during every dark of the moons, to exchange spells and secrets.

...that princes and princesses visited in disguise, for secret assignations or private negotiations. Possibly with those wizards or thieves or so-called adventurers.

...that half of the building was actually built underground, where they serviced clientele from those peoples who lived beneath the surface of the world. Both the good ones and the bad ones.

And on and on and on the stories went.

In some ways, the idea that the occasional murder happened there and got covered up was almost the *least* of the things I'd heard about the Purple Gryphon.

Yes, of course, I knew that some of the Bendsfolk would come here to drink sometimes, and leave saying it was just another inn. Maybe with better music.

But then, those Bendsfolk only ever described the main room, just inside the front doors, under the Purple Gryphon sign. They never said anything about the upstairs, or any of the rest of just what anyone could see from the outside.

Which told me that maybe they hadn't seen any more than they'd been allowed to see.

No, I didn't think that meant the rumors were true. But it meant one or more of them might be. And the possibilities fascinated me.

Honestly, I was surprised that half the youths my age weren't lining up to work there.

The Purple Gryphon itself had started as a single, two-story building. Or so I'd heard from my parents, and I didn't have any reason to doubt them. Wide and broad, even then, but only the two stories.

Approaching that cool spring morning under the slowly brightening dawn, I thought I could *just* make out the bones of that original building. It had all been river stone, and held together with heathy smearings of mortar. Windows framed and shuttered with good maple, and painted pale purple, like the gryphon on the sign.

Oh, but the Purple Gryphon was much bigger now. Four stories high in the front, six high in the back, and it looked to have stretched its arms – or maybe it's claws – out to the side for more room.

The main building still looked to be all river stone, including the little tower jutting up in the front right corner, as I faced it that morning. Though the upper levels had browner stone to them, I thought, and were fitted better than the two lower stories. Didn't need as much mortar to hold them together. Same purple-painted maple for the window shutters, too.

And out to the sides, mostly wooden and two-story over what looked to be river stone foundations. Darker purple, with light purple trim.

The right side kind of curled back around as it neared the old apothecary shop, curving toward Gryphon's stables. The left side stretched near on to fifty paces before it split into three tines. Like someone had taken a pitchfork and bent the outside tines down to be perpendicular with the handle.

Maybe a dozen chimneys jutted up through the cobbled roof at various points.

The whole building was vast and chaotic and beautiful in a way I couldn't put into words. Maybe just because it seemed to contain infinite possibilities, even for a farm boy like me.

I made my way all the way around to the back, where the stables were the largest in town. Wider and deeper all on their own than maybe even the original building had been.

I had to smile at the smell. Even the horses smelled better here. Oh, not their leavings, of course, and there was plenty of that odor to the air too, but I'd grown up on a farm. I knew well how to set aside that smell for the better ones hiding underneath. And those horses smelled sweet as the spring river water.

Workers were already busy in those stables. I could hear the stablemaster giving orders to his hands, and the sound of a working pitchfork that I knew all too well.

I passed by the stables, and headed for the three stone steps at the back that led to the wide purple door that had to lead to the kitchen. I could smell breads and pastries baking as I approached.

Like Dad had told me to do, I knocked three times with strong, sure beats. So the sound would carry, and imply that I meant business.

I'd barely finished my third knock when the door whipped open.

"You're late already, you— Oh!"

My breath caught as I saw her. Older than me by a few years, but not too many. Bright blue eyes, hair soft as cornsilk, falling in curls a man could get lost in.

Pretty didn't begin to do her justice.

"Well?" she said, amused now and one eyebrow high. "You're obviously not Kean with the lamb. So did you want something? Or just to stand there staring at me?"

I forced myself to swallow, and wedged out words past the sunburn-level heat in my face.

"I would like a job."

Her voice gentled a little as she said, "Try the stables, farm boy. They may have work for you."

I shook my head. "I could tend animals on the farm. I want to work here. Inside."

She leaned one shoulder against the doorframe, and I tried hard not to let my eyes stray to the neckline of that dark purple dress she wore under her apron.

"Oh, you do, do you?" she asked, and I'd like to think her tone was playful, not mocking. "And just what do you think you could do for us?"

"Whatever needs doing," I said firmly.

"Laren! No time for your flirting now." That was a stern, older voice, and I could hear its owner approaching, even as I now felt so hot I might've jumped into a summer's eve bonfire to cool down.

"I wasn't flirting, ma'am," Laren said. "This boy says he wants a job."

I saw the older woman now. Clearly the woman who ran the

kitchen. She had the build of a lifelong cook who enjoyed tasting her wares. And she looked to have the kind of strength in her thick arms that she could have slung a whole pig over one shoulder to carry it inside for butchering.

She shooed Laren back into the kitchen, and frowned from the shoulders up as she looked me over.

"You Sonnal's boy?"

"Yes, ma'am," I said.

"Thought as much. You've got her fair hair and eyes, her cheeks and her chin, but you can thank the gods you took your build from that man she married. Good shoulders. You'll have good muscles someday."

I didn't say anything while she looked me over again.

"You already try the stables?"

"No, ma'am. I could work with animals at home. I want to work *here*. Inside."

"And why do you want a fool thing like that?"

"Any other trade, I learn a trade. Here, I learn people. And maybe a number of trades."

"What do you think goes on in here, boy?"

"People drink. Eat. Talk. Sleep. Sing. Dance. Gamble, maybe."

She nodded, and at the time, I thought her nod was approval. As though I'd given the smart answer, and hadn't been caught up in the thousand thousand rumors about the place.

Looking back, though, I see that nod for what it was. That I'd given her the answer she expected. Which meant I didn't really know. Which, of course, I couldn't possibly.

She nodded again, though, and this time she'd made a decision.

"You'll do as your told?"

"Yes, ma'am."

"Not going to shy away from getting your hands dirty?"

"No, ma'am."

"You can keep a secret?"

"As many as I need to," I said, excitement bubbling up inside me now.

"All right," she said with one more nod. "Offer you the same deal you'd get anywhere else, then. We'll try you and see how you work out. And we'll give you room and board, and a small stipend that will grow as you do. Assuming you prove yourself."

"I will, ma'am, and thank you."

"Save your thanks. You may need them later."

———

THAT WAS TEN YEARS AGO, THE DAY I FIRST WALKED INSIDE THE PURPLE Gryphon.

Yinda, defying odds that would beggar any gambler, not only got accepted as an apprentice by Bolan, the town blacksmith, she *thrived*. She outstripped the other apprentices, and was the first of the lot to make journeyman.

She had some muscle to her now, but it wasn't her strength that made her so good. It was her precision. She had a better gauge of the heats that metals responded to than any of her fellows, and a better eye for what metals could take, and what they needed.

I saw her at the end of every market day, when we'd share a meal and catch up on our lives. Not that I could tell her all that much.

I wasn't supposed to talk about anything that went on inside the Purple Gryphon. Which in some ways, was funny, because so much of it was the same kind of thing that happened in every inn or tavern.

People ate and drank and talked. They sang and danced. They gambled. They took each other into private places, for meetings or assignations or both.

And there were many private places tucked away inside the Purple Gryphon. Not just the upstairs rooms where people *slept*, as well as engaged in other private activities. I mean that the main building itself, as well as its wings – and I was told early on to call them wings, not arms or claws – had many secret rooms that people could rent for any number of reasons. Rooms that were every bit as busy as the main room that most visiting Bendsfolk saw.

And that wasn't all.

At least some of the rumors about the place were true.

Oh, not the murders, of course. In all ten years I'd worked there to that point, I'd never heard of anyone getting murdered at the Purple Gryphon. Or even leaving without paying, for that matter.

No, I mean that wizards did gather there to eat and drink and talk. Real wizards, I mean, not just fakers. I sometimes got to see them cast little spells. Mostly small illusions, to go with some story they were telling one another.

And those so-called adventurers? They came to the Purple Gryphon in droves. Men and women who looked as comfortable carrying swords and maces and axes as my father did with a hoe. And some of the wizards traveled with them. And priests too, men and women both, dedicated to one god or other or sometimes several at once, to judge by the holy sigils they wore proudly.

Sometimes they came in haggard and road weary. Sometimes they needed healers. Sometimes they came in flush with coin and laughter. And sometimes they huddled around old maps or strange scrolls or books.

It was one of those adventurers who changed my life.

Now, I wasn't a blacksmith like Yinda, but in the ten years I'd worked at the Purple Gryphon, I'd filled out more than a little myself. Whether it was toting around barrels of ale or mead or wine or savra, or framing and repairing furniture that got smashed during the occasional brawl, or one of the other of the many, many tasks they found for me, I'd had more than enough cause to pack on muscle the way a merchant packs his cart for travel.

I'd grown taller too, by a good three handspans, and though I still couldn't grow a proper beard – kept myself clean shaven for that reason – there must've been something about my looks the women liked. Because by that point, even Laren flirted with me now and then.

Not that she meant anything by it. She'd married Poli, the chief stable hand, and was always talking about how they'd quit as soon as they saved enough to open that bake shop she was always talking about.

In fact, I remember that just before everything started that night, Laren was complaining to me, quietly and off to one side of the blazing kitchen. There was this little spot between the stairs down to the meat cellar and the entry to the vegetable pantry where the open doors kind of made a little alcove, up against the river stone wall. Perfect for a quick word out from under the watchful eye of Beka, who ran the kitchen.

Laren soured the wonderful smells of bread and pheasant with the news that Poli had lost their money gambling. Again.

Poor Poli. He had a great head for horses. But as good as he was with mares, geldings and stallions, he was just as bad at knucklebones.

Now, Laren liked to complain to me – quietly, and with no one listening – because I'd more than proven over the years that I could keep a secret. But something was different about the way she was complaining that night. She looked and sounded so *sad*, you might've thought her mom had died.

And I could understand. This was at least the third time he'd done it, just since she'd started telling me. Oh, maybe a year ago, give or take a season.

I felt like I needed to say or do something. Only problem was, I'd learned a lot about keeping my mouth *shut*, but not a lot about what to *say* when people were in trouble. And the only thing I could think to *do* was offer her a hug, which just sounded like a terrible idea. Her being married and me not being her husband.

Frankly, even patting her on the shoulder might've been the wrong move, especially since there wasn't half an arm span between us. But I'd been just about to do that anyway when Kue Rinton stepped into the kitchen.

If at least half of the rumors about the Purple Gryphon were true, then at least two-thirds of the rumors about Kue Rinton were true.

Purple eyes? Oh, yes. A vivid, pale purple color, those eyes. Gave me a shiver every time I met them, because I swear I could feel her looking straight through me. And I don't just mean down to my bones. I mean, every time Kue Rinton looked at me, I felt like she could see every thought I'd ever had. Knew about every little thing I'd ever done.

All of it.

Like she could see every bit of good and bad there was to a person, and she weighed and measured you with every look.

Was she a witch? Well, I didn't know that. But I didn't have any trouble believing she had some magic to her. Never did seem to get any older. I mean, that night when she walked into the kitchen while I'd been talking with Laren in the fake alcove, Kue Rinton looked just the same as she had the day I'd started working there.

That vivid black hair. That smooth skin that was tanned as any farmer's, though she never spent much time outside.

And that rumor that she'd had a thousand lovers, well, I didn't know about that. But she certainly had her share of admirers, men and women both.

I wasn't one of them, though. Never could get past those eyes.

Another rumor I was never sure about, was the one that said Kue Rinton could be whatever size she wanted. I mean, from the day I'd stopped growing, I didn't remember ever seeing her any taller or shorter than about my rib cage. And she was always on the slender side.

Have to say, though. When she got angry, it was like she filled the whole room so tight there wasn't even space for air.

So there I was, in that little fake alcove of the kitchen. Laren all misty and sad over what her husband had done. My fool hand just starting to lift towards her shoulder. When—

"Zian." Kue Rinton just said my name. That was all. No special kind of tone or anything.

And yet, my hand stopped moving and I all but forgot Laren was there as I turned my head and saw Kue Rinton, standing across the kitchen at just the perfect angle to see me in that fake alcove, but maybe not see Laren.

Out of the corner of my eye, I could see that Laren's eyes had rounded, and any threat of tears just vanished from her face. She looked like she'd been caught doing something wrong, even though all we'd been doing was talking.

The conversation was over though. Kue Rinton was not someone to keep waiting.

I hadn't noticed how empty the kitchen had been until I was crossing it right then. Beka came back in from the meat cellar, carrying a side of beef. And the other kitchen hands ... well, I didn't know what they were up to. But usually there were three or four in the kitchen most times, and just then the only one was Laren.

When I reached Kue Rinton, I ducked my head and said, "Ma'am," as I always did.

She frowned at me a moment. Shook her head.

"You know where I keep the Lava Rock Ale?"

Had to think a moment, but she gave me that moment. Once I'd gotten big enough to carry up a barrel, I'd been given a half-day to learn the layout of the bar cellars. Did a good job of it, when the bartenders tested me, but it had been a long time ago. And I'd never had to fetch the Lava Rock Ale before.

I nodded. "I think so, ma'am. Second room. Back wall. Got a sigil like a black mountain with a red top."

"That's the one," she said. "Fetch one of the half-barrels and bring it to private room twelve."

"Yes, ma'am." I started to turn away, but she cleared her throat, so I looked back at her.

"You've been a good lad so far," she said, then looked off toward that fake alcove, then back at me. And there was something in her eyes I couldn't read. "You stay that way now. Hear me?"

"Yes, ma'am," I said.

"Off you go."

THE BAR CELLARS WERE JUST ONE PART OF THE UNDERGROUND SECTION of the Purple Gryphon. Really was a warren down there of private rooms, sitting rooms, and even a duplicate of the main room above it, which I'd never seen in full swing.

It got used though. I knew, because I'd helped clean it up more than once. And I'd had to repair or rebuild furniture for it too.

In fact, though, I never really went into any of the underground areas as part of my work. Except to do what I was doing then – bringing an occasional half-barrel of something special to a private gathering.

A half-barrel usually meant a dozen or so drinkers, getting ready to have some kind of party.

Private room twelve was a little small for that kind of group, but maybe they were friendly enough they wouldn't care. Rather spend a little more on their specialty ale, instead of where they drank it. So long as it was private enough to suit them.

And all the underground rooms felt private as a tomb.

No dirt floors down there. Oh, no. It was all river stone, mortared into place, with stone pillars for supports in the bigger rooms.

Always colder down there than upstairs. And maybe it was because I knew all that rock came from the river, but it always felt just a little ... moist down there. Like there should've been moss growing on the rocks, or at least mildew, but I never smelled any.

The rock had its own kind of smell, though. Like it carried a memory of the river inside it, and only let out enough that passersby would know where it came from.

Had to carry an oil lamp with me. No sconces for candles, away from the kitchen and bar cellars. Any group that needed an underground room got a lamp and a guide to lead them there, and then meet them again to guide them out when their time was up.

Always thought that was strange, but I suppose it discouraged guests wandering off where they weren't supposed to. Or at least made them obvious, if they did. Assuming they had any light of their own.

When I got to the door to private room twelve – not numbered or anything, of course – I set down the lamp and knocked.

Just about the time I was crouched down to pick up the lamp, the door opened and I was staring eye-to-eye with a craggy face. Great big round nose, bent from having been broken at least twice. Neatly trimmed brown beard in the shape of a hammer on the right cheek, and an axe on the left. Otherwise, clean shaven as me.

"This a joke, boy?" he growled at me in a deeper voice than I would've expected from a man roughly the same height as Kue Rinton.

"Sir?" I asked, confused, and stuck staring into those dark hazel eyes. My free hand too close to the lamp and on the verge of getting burnt, but I didn't feel like I could move.

I'd realized by now that this man was wearing full chain mail made from some dark metal, over a build as thick with muscle as any blacksmith's.

"I said," he leaned close enough that his nose poked mine. "Is this your idea of a joke?"

"I ... I ... I..." Try as I might, I couldn't understand how I'd offended this man. But he sure looked ready to hit me, and I was hardly in a position to defend myself, since I was carrying...

"Ale," I said hopefully, moving the half-barrel tucked under my left arm to try to draw attention to it.

"Ease off, Ig," an amused woman's voice said. "He's just the house man with our ale."

"He hasn't answered my question."

"Don't be a fool." This speaker sounded like an irritated, older man. "Can't you see you caught him trying to pick up his lamp?"

"Then why hasn't he picked it up?"

"Because you've scared him half to death." This speaker's tone was flat. Not just matter of fact, but strangely flat. As though adding intonation while speaking never occurred to them.

"You just reaching for your lamp, boy?" the man in front of me – Ig, apparently – asked.

I nodded.

"Then pick it up and bring in our ale before I go outside and drink your river dry."

Ig growled something I didn't understand, but moved out of my way and gave me an impatient gesture that might've been an invitation to enter.

"I would advise you to do as he says," the affectless speaker said. "Ig lacks patience when he thirsts."

"That's putting it mildly," the woman said, still sounding amused by everything that had happened so far.

"I'll just pick it up on my way out," I said, straightening and stepping into the room, closing the door behind me.

Private room twelve was only about five paces across, both ways. Had a round, oak table that took up most of the room, but it also had a fireplace, with a gentle, cherrywood fire popping and driving away the chill.

No decorations in the room except for one shelf that held a half-barrel and six wooden mugs. The walls had three candles each, in iron sconces, that lit the room comfortably.

The other three speakers were seated around that table

The older man was more than a little older. Long hair and a full beard, both black shot through with gray. Heavyset, but he wore silks that had been tailored to make him look good. Red for the shirt, dark purple for the...

Where those hose? I'd heard of hose, but never seen them before. They certainly looked too thin to be breeches.

The woman was about my age, and decked out all in leather. She was twirling a thin, double-edged dagger in her left hand, and looking me over like she was inspecting a horse at market. She was smiling as she did those things, but honestly I was too scared to notice if she was pretty or not. I know she did wear her dark hair pulled back in a tight braid.

The other had to have been the affectless speaker. Also clad all in leather, but where the woman's leathers were dark – almost black – this person's leathers were paler. Like undyed buckskin, maybe.

Couldn't tell how old this person was, or even if they were male or female. Tanned skin – even more so than the others, who weren't exactly pale themselves – hair that blue color at the root of a flame, and eyes close to amber.

I realized then that among their packs against the wall, they carried weapons. A couple of swords, a war hammer, a battle axe, a bow, and around that point I swallowed and went about my business.

I pulled down the empty barrel, tapped the new one, and filled five mugs before hoisting it onto its little shelf.

I brought the first two mugs to Ig, which got an amused, "Ha!" from the woman. I then started passing out the others.

I got to the woman last, and when I did she met my eye with a saucy smile. She said, "Thanks, handsome," then gave me a wink and pinched my bottom.

I'd heard of that happening to some of the servers, but I'd never been a server before. I didn't know how to react. Was I supposed to object? Smile and flirt? I'd heard of servers doing both...

Instead, I turned away, feeling my face go hot from embarrassment, and noticed that in the middle of the table they'd laid out an old map. Old enough that Terand's Bend wasn't even present as a nameless spot for a landmark.

But I knew our river, and the distance to the mountains, and I knew where the waterfall fell...

"That waterfall's not there anymore," I said, without thinking. "Hasn't been since before my grandmother's grandmother's time."

They all four stared at me, and every bit of heat I'd felt in my face fled, leaving a chill in its wake.

"I ... I'm sorry," I said, pulling my hands back. "I don't mean to pry. I should leave you to your business."

"Wait!" the old man snapped, and when he did, the candles all flared brighter.

Dyaphane's Blood! Not only were these four adventurers, but that one was a *wizard*.

I was a dead man. I was sure of it. My body just didn't know it yet.

"I'm *sorry*," I said again, now backing toward the nearest wall. "I can't read any of the writing. I don't know—"

"I'd say he knows more than we do about some things," the affectless speaker said.

"All of you shut up," the woman said, getting out of her chair so she stood between me and the rest of them. She raised her hands and soothed with her voice like I was a spooked sheep she wanted to calm. She even locked eyes with me. Hers were a dark shade of green.

"It's all right, handsome," she said. "You're among friends. Duron didn't mean to spook you. He just gets excited about new knowledge. Like Ig there gets excited about good ale. You know what it's like to get excited, don't you?"

I nodded, feeling more like a spooked sheep than I wanted to admit.

"Of course you do," she said with a smile. Not a teasing smile this time. More like I was someone she was happy to meet. And she didn't close in on me either, like she was afraid I'd bolt if I felt penned in. "I'm Qala," she said. "What's your name?"

"Zian. Zian Sonnalsson."

"That naming style is consistent with the faming communities in this region," the affectless speaker said.

"We've already established he's local, Edan," she said in a warning tone, before softening her voice as she spoke to me again.

"Well it's a pleasure to meet you, Zian. That's Edan." Qala nodded toward Edan without breaking eye contact with me. "Edan gets excited about new animals and creatures. Unfortunately that often includes new communities of humans, but don't take it personally."

I nodded, caught between wondering what Edan was and deciding that maybe I wasn't a dead man just yet.

***

My back hit the cold stone of the wall. My feet penned between packs and weapons. Qala not much more than a pace away. Smiling like I was an old friend. Or at least a welcome new friend.

The other three watched from their seats at the table.

Ig glared impatiently, fidgeting with his mug. As though maybe still deciding whether or not to take insult at my accidentally meeting him at eye level.

Duron watched me with interest, fingers steepled, as though waiting for me to do some kind of trick.

Edan, well, I wasn't sure how to interpret what I saw in those amber eyes, but it had to have been curiosity, at least.

My heart was still pounding, and my shoulders were still in knots, but I was calming down. The danger moment seemed to have passed. I started to move toward the door, but wasn't sure how to get past the pack to my right without tripping on that big battle axe.

"Whoa there, handsome," Qala said, putting a halting hand on my near shoulder, and taking me by the elbow with the other. "Easy. Don't go just yet."

"We have questions we would like you to answer," Edan said, and from the frown on Duron's face, he'd been trying to think of a gentler way to ask the same question.

"Come join us for a drink," Qala said, giving her companions a quick glare, before smiling at me again. "And maybe you can tell us a little about the area."

"I'm not supposed to drink with the customers," I said, but I found myself guided to the round, oak table all the same, right beside Qala's chair. And her hand had moved to my other shoulder, so she now had an arm around me, while her near hand gave my upper arm an appraising squeeze.

"We won't tell if you don't," Qala said with a wink. "Have a seat."

"Please, no," I said, gesturing to the chair. "You should sit."

"All that," Qala said, her smile getting teasing again as she slid her hands off me and reclaimed her seat, "and polite, too."

Ig scoffed.

Wasn't politeness, actually. If there'd been an extra chair, I'd've sat in it. But she was a customer and I wasn't. So the last chair had to go to her.

Didn't figure my best move was pointing that out, though.

"Now," Duron said, pointing at the spot on the map where there was supposed to be a waterfall. "We have been to the waterfall near your village and not found what we were looking for. You suggest that the waterfall is someplace *other* than where it is indicated here?"

"Because the rock shapes around the waterfall are *right*," Ig said, and he looked as though he'd been having this argument with Duron for some time before I came in.

"And yet," Duron said, some anger flaring in his tone, "more than one rock may have the right shape."

Qala let out a whistle that was too loud and too sharp that room. Everyone winced but her and Edan.

"If I might remind you two worthies," she said, and maybe it was just my imagination, but I thought she made "worthies" sound a little sarcastic, "we have a local here who might know something more about this region than our map tells us."

Qala turned her smile on me again. "Now then, handsome, what were you saying before about the waterfall?"

"Well," I said, then swallowed. "If you ask me, I think your mapmaker drew those mountains before he followed the river. Because their shapes are right enough, more or less, but they aren't quite to the same scale as the river and the valley floor."

"I believe I said as much several days ago," Edan said.

"And *some*one said that didn't matter because he knew the rock shapes," Duron said.

Qala cleared her throat noisily.

The others looked at her, and then at me.

"See," I said, pointing to a spot along the mountainside, following the valley scale. "That's where the waterfall comes down these days. River comes down through here to join with the map river here." I pointed to the right spot, if I was gauging the distances right. "Far as I know, we never found out what made it change its course, up in the mountains."

"I could speculate," Edan began, but Qala hushed him.

"And the waterfall on the map," Qala said. "The old waterfall. Do you know where that would be?"

"Oh, yeah. There's a nice little cave under where the falls used to be. My friends and I would use it as a base when we went hunting farther afield. About a ... day and a half from here, hiking."

They all looked at each other.

"I could probably draw you a corrected trail..." I said, trailing off because I felt unsure that was entirely true. Looking more at the map now, I thought it was off. That looked like more than a day and a half to hike to that waterfall spot.

"But *you* know how to get there?" Ig asked.

"Well, yeah," I said. "Me and about a third of the people in town, I expect."

"But *you* know," Duron said.

"And you possess muscles that suggest you could handle yourself," Edan said.

"Well, I've had to scrap a *couple* of times, yeah, but—"

"Have you ever used a sword?" Ig asked.

"Well, not a real one—"

Qala whistled again. I couldn't help but wonder why Edan didn't wince.

"What my friends here are trying to say, handsome, is that we would appreciate the pleasure of your company on a small excursion." She smiled and patted my arm appreciatively, then gave it a small squeeze. "Me especially."

She fluttered her lashes at me, and I was suddenly very aware of just how pretty she was. Her eyes, her cheekbones, her long, slender throat. Her skin so smooth, except for that little scar near the tip of her chin.

"I ... I have work..."

"I'll go talk to Kue," Duron said, standing and heading for the door.

"Any excuse will do for that," Ig taunted him, but immediately turned his attention back to me. And he looked ... hungry.

"We will, of course, compensate you for your time and efforts," Edan said. "So do not concern yourself with the monetary end of the question."

"Come on, handsome," Qala said. "It'll be fun. And if it all works out, maybe you and I can celebrate, afterwards. Just the two of us."

Now, working in a place like the Purple Gryphon, I'd had my share of offers in the past. Even accepted a few of them.

But Qala wasn't like any woman I'd ever met before. Her sheer *confidence*. I definitely liked the idea of spending more time around her.

Plus, well, I knew it was risky. But I'd been looking for action and excitement when I first came to work at the Purple Gryphon.

And this looked to be the most exciting thing that had ever happened to me. By far.

I NEVER DID ACCEPT THAT DRINK. FAR AS I WAS CONCERNED, I WAS STILL working. But standing there in that little private meeting room, I told those four adventurers everything I knew about the area where the waterfall used to be. Unfortunately, what I knew didn't seem to cover any of the things they wanted to know.

See, the cave under the old falls? I think they were expecting it to be the kind of cave that led into a network of tunnels. But it just wasn't that kind of cave.

Honestly, even calling it a cave was kind of giving it a compliment. Wasn't particularly *deep*, or anything. More like a gentle indentation in the rock, than a proper cave.

Still, I mean, it was a good place for a handful of friends to find shelter for their fire while hunting. Not much more than that, though.

I could at least tell them about the animals that frequented the area. The larger ones, that is. I didn't figure they needed to hear about the mice and voles and rabbits and such.

Instead, I told them all about the habits of the mountain goats that sometimes ventured low enough to make good hunting. About the elk that often came down early in the spring, a little skinnier from their winter diet, but a little slower, and with thicker pelts.

I warned them about the hill cats we had to watch out for, especially when the elk came down. Not because the cats would attack *us* so much as steal our kills. Or any food we brought along.

I told them which birds were good to hear nearby, and which

ones were just as bad as the mountain cats about trying to steal your food or your kill, if it was small enough.

In other words, I told them all the kinds of things *I'd* needed to know to hunt the area properly.

But then they started asking about creatures I didn't know anything about. The kinds I'd only even heard of as rumors told by travelers. And such rumors were always suspect.

Kolks? Ne-rinde? Those things that were said to walk like men, but might come up from the world below to slaughter and pillage?

They were as distant and unreal as the border wars I'd heard about as a child, and felt even less likely to be true. I'd certainly never seen nor heard of any such things anywhere near Terand's Bend.

So no matter how many times Ig and Duron asked about Kolks and Ne-rinde, or how many *ways* they asked, there wasn't really anything I could tell them. Finally it took Qala and Edan both to convince the other two that I wouldn't know "the signs" if I saw them. That such things were simply too far outside my experience.

Finally, though, they finished making their plans. The five of us would arise before dawn – no feat for me, I did it every day, but Qala and Duron seemed unhappy about the prospect – see about outfitting me for the journey, and we'd be on our way.

Then the four of them were ready to retire to their rooms. And though Qala teased a little more, she didn't invite me to join her.

Just as well. I'd've been tempted to do so, but I knew full well that I had to talk to Kue Rinton. Duron could tell me all night that he'd spoken to her and that she'd given her permission for me to take time away from work to travel with them, but I needed to hear it from her myself.

So, once I and my lamp had guided the four adventurers to the main room – which was still going strong with cheers and singing and drinking – I set off to find the Purple Gryphon's owner.

I didn't have to look long. She was waiting for me back behind the bar. Caught me with her eyes and nodded toward a door I'd never seen the other side of.

Some of the staff said that she kept offices in three parts of the

Purple Gryphon. I didn't know if that was true or not. The only office I knew about was the one back behind the bar in the main room.

Just looking at that door felt like a violation. As though my eyes were doing something wrong by noticing it, and immediately I felt the urge to look away. At anything else. Even the scarred visage of one-eyed Old Nik, our bartender, was preferable to looking at the door to Kue Rinton's office.

And now I was invited into it?

Gave me that itchy feeling all over my skin. Like I'd already worked up a sweat on the farm *before* I had to bale taro all afternoon and got stickers all over.

But I screwed up my courage and I stepped up beside her as she opened the door exactly enough for the two of us to slip through before closing it again.

Thankfully, the room was already lit. Two candles in iron sconces along the river stone of each wall. The room was a little wider than it was deep. Maybe six paces wide, and four across. But it kept going up.

Instead of a ceiling where I expected to see one, there was a broad wooden walkway, with support beams coming down to the first floor walls.

Couldn't tell what was up there, though. It was black as pitch, as though the candlelight from down here was scared of what it might see.

And there wasn't any ladder, or any stairs, or any way of getting up there that I could see.

"You don't need to worry about what's up there," Kue Rinton said. "We're staying down here right now."

"Right, ma'am," I said, ducking my head to her. "Sorry."

"No reason to be sorry," she said, taking a seat behind a small desk made from some kind of reddish wood I didn't recognize. There were no other chairs in the room, but each of the supports for that walkway also formed the frame of a set of ash wood cabinets. And there was a table behind her desk that looked like she experimented with spices, and with brewing on a small scale. All kinds of little jars and vials, a couple of mortars and pestles, that kind of thing.

Or maybe that was witchy stuff. I didn't know.

I did know that the room smelled like some combination of herbs I couldn't quite place. I knew all the plants that grew around Terand's Bend pretty well, but what I smelled in that room wasn't any of them. It was a sharper smell, and slightly bitter. Couldn't imagine what plant could make it.

By the time I realized I'd let my eyes wander, I also realized that Kue Rinton was watching me. Patiently. Expectantly, even.

"You're having quite a day, aren't you?" she asked.

"I didn't mean to pester the customers, ma'am."

"What did you mean to do, Zian?"

"I..." I cleared my throat. Told her what I'd been doing when the door opened and how Ig had taken offense and how the others had started arguing about it. "...and so I figured I'd pour their first round – two mugs for Ig – and then that Qala pinched my ... well..."

"Yes, I imagine she did. Go on."

"Well, I didn't know what I was supposed to do, ma'am. I mean, they were paying customers and all, and I'd already come close to insulting one of them. So I figured, best to just ignore it and go. But as I turned I saw they had a map, but it was old. And not so accurate as a map should be. And before I knew it I'd mentioned that the waterfall by the little cross someone had drawn wasn't where the waterfall was anymore, and—"

"Ah," she said with a nod. "So *that's* why they asked for you. They wanted a local guide. One of the Bendsfolk. And that Duron tried to tell me they wanted you as a porter."

"Well, two of them – Ig and Edan – did mention maybe having me tote some stuff for them."

"All the same," she said firmly, "a guide should command a higher rate than a simple porter." Her small nostrils flared in irritation. "I won't stand for them trying to cheat you. I'll see to it that before you depart in the morning, they leave a sufficient deposit for you. To retain your services as a guide for, shall we say, a week? With a small additional amount if they expect you to act as a porter, as well."

"Thank you, ma'am," I said.

"Not at all." She waved away my thanks. "You've been a good worker, and so far, a good man. I will not have my people cheated. And there is more. If they should retrieve a lost treasure of some sort, you should be entitled to a half-share of its value, on top of any other fees."

"I should?"

"Most definitely," she said with a nod. "They could recover nothing without you or they wouldn't be hiring you. And they plan to outfit you for the journey, yes?"

"They're talking about buying me some armor. And a weapon. Not that they expect me to fight, but—"

"But once you're out there, the fight may come to you and you should be ready. That is proper."

She looked at me closely, and I once more felt those purple eyes boring inside me.

"Are you sure you want to do this, Zian?"

I blinked and shivered away that sensation. "Ma'am?"

"That Qala is fetching enough, I'll grant you. But if she's the reason you're doing this, you shouldn't. She's the type to play with you once or twice and cast you aside. Not out of any intentional cruelty, you understand. But because she has a wandering nature and will not bind herself to any man, any woman, or any place."

"Hadn't really thought that far, ma'am."

"I imagine not. At your age, thinking can be tricky when staring into certain kinds of eyes."

And then she actually smiled. *Kue Rinton* smiled. Couldn't remember if I'd ever seen her smile before, but she smiled then. A friendly kind of smile. Maybe even the fondness of a memory.

It was so unexpected that I missed what she said then, and had to ask her to repeat it.

She chuckled. "I asked you *why* you want to do this? If not to win Qala's heart, why? The money, perhaps?"

I got as far as an embarrassed, sheepish kind of smile before she answered for me.

"Ah. Looking for a little excitement, is it? The call to adventure?"

"Well, I don't know about any call, ma'am, but I've never done anything like this, and it does sound exciting."

She gave a gentle snort. "Then I hope you enjoy yourself. But more than that, I hope you survive what you're looking for, Zian."

"Ma'am?"

"They're buying you armor. What does that tell you?"

"That I might need it." Cold realization washed down through me. I swallowed hard.

"*There*," she said, and nodded. "*That* was what I wanted to see. I don't mind your going, and your job will be here when you return, if you still want it. But I couldn't let you go without making sure you really understood what the risks were."

"Thank you, ma'am."

"Of course." She leaned forward. "And Zian, now that you understand what you're in for, if you'd like to change your mind, *you can*. Just tell me right now, or sleep on it and tell me first thing in the morning. You won't be in any trouble for it. I'll see to that. And you won't have to tell *them* you've changed your mind. I'll take care of that. And I'll find them another guide, so you won't have to worry that you're leaving them in the lurch."

You know, it's funny. I think that in the ten years I'd worked there, I'd held Kue Rinton in awe, and maybe feared her a little. Probably rightly, to be honest. But that moment right then was the first time I realized that, she really did care about us. We who worked for her.

And I'm pretty sure that understanding was in my eyes when I looked up at her then.

"Thank you, ma'am. But I think I want to do this."

"All right. Go turn in then. You'll have an early day of it. And remember what I said."

"I will, ma'am. And thank you."

Didn't sleep much that night. But I didn't change my mind, either.

THE ONLY THING I HAD TO PACK IN THE MORNING WAS CLOTHES. THEY promised they'd handle the rest. Bedroll and food and so forth. They even had me join them in the main room for breakfast before we set out.

Don't know what I was expecting at that breakfast, but it wasn't what I got.

Not the food. I mean, they didn't want any kind of porridge or stew, so we ate leftover roast chicken from the night before, with bread and honey and water. (Except for Ig, who insisted loudly that water only existed for washing, and had ale instead.)

No, it's just. I guess I expected them to ... welcome me or something. But they didn't.

Ig acknowledged me with a grunt, but since he didn't look like he wanted to hit me, I figured that was all right.

Edan only nodded their head at me. Which, again, wasn't much, but it wasn't aggressive, either.

Qala didn't greet me at all. She kind of hunched in on herself, didn't make eye contact with anyone, and didn't do much more than growl when she wanted more food or water. And when whatever she wanted was passed to her, she snatched with hands so fast I barely saw them.

Duron snarled at me, so I gave him a little extra space, to be safe. And he didn't participate in the conversation. Of which there was little. Mostly Edan and Ig, chatting in a guttural language I didn't speak. Edan spoke with no inflection in that language either.

Thought that was kind of rude, but under the circumstances, I didn't think saying anything was the smart way to go.

So I ate and drank quietly, trying to watch the others without looking like I was watching them. That was always easy to do when I was working, because so few people paid attention to the workers at a place like the Purple Gryphon, unless we were serving them. They were too busy paying attention to each other.

But doing so while sitting there at the big bench table with them that wasn't so easy.

At that hour, the main room of the Purple Gryphon felt like the room itself was sleeping off last night's indulgence. No one stood at the big, long bar, demanding service. No one stood *behind* the bar either, for that matter. Not for service. Just Ontee, cleaning up and double-checking last night's final count, in terms of bottles and barrels.

The eight large benches in the middle of the room were mostly empty. Just two groups. Me and the adventurers, in the near corner, under the tapestry of a wolf pack stalking a foolish hunter. Across the room and over two tables, so they could be in front of the freshly rekindled hearth, six merchants chattered and argued in Zalanese.

I didn't understand much Zalanese, but I knew enough to know they were debating the costs and profits of ... trade routes following some big to-do down south.

There were a few scattered diners on their lonesome, either with big bench tables all to themselves, or parked at one of the little round tables under the windows, which were still shuttered as yet.

Three of them I figured for messengers preparing for a long day in the saddle. The other four, I thought, looked like soldiers in search of a battle. Not that they'd find one near Terand's Bend.

And, of course, Alton and Malay bringing out more food and drinks, when called for.

Alton and Malay kept giving me smiles, but I was too nervous to smile back. Especially the way my companions were behaving. No, it was far more important that I try to study these four. Learn all I could about them. Preferably without them realizing I was doing so.

Mostly that meant keeping my focus on my plate, while paying attention to what I could see from the corner of my eye.

Ig and Edan were involved in their discussion. But they both seemed lively enough – well, Ig seemed lively, Edan I wasn't sure about – and acting much the way they had the night before.

Over the course of breakfast, Qala slowly sort of unfolded herself. Food seemed to help. And once the hot tea was poured, that helped even more.

There'd been some debate about that. The hot tea. Ig hadn't

wanted to bother, but both Duron and Qala had snapped at his objection, and Edan had played peacemaker.

Tea seemed to pour a little life into Qala, and it soothed whatever was rankling Duron's nerves. Neither one of them participated in the conversation – which I was starting to think was about what they expected to find – but they didn't growl and snarl so much.

By the time the group was ready to leave, Qala even gave me a wink. It wasn't much, as winks go, but it was better than getting growled at. Even came with a ghost of her usual smile.

We didn't go out the front, as I'd expected us to. I started that way, but Ig laughed at me.

"I'm not walking all the way around to get to my horse, boy."

"His name is Zian," Edan said, voice still as affectless as ever. "If he is man enough to guide us, he is man enough to be called by his name."

Ig snorted, but nodded.

I half-expected some kind of saucy comment from Qala, but she ignored the exchange, already on her way toward the back, with Duron.

We passed the kitchen entrance on our way out, and Laren stood in the doorway, giving me a wistful kind of look, brow furrowed and lips pulled in. But she didn't say anything, or even wave goodbye. So I just gave her a little wave as I passed.

SKY WAS JUST LIGHTENING TOWARD DAWN WHEN WE GOT OUTSIDE. Not so much chill to the air as I expected though. Or maybe I was just warm from excitement.

Poli glared at me while bringing out the horses, but he didn't say anything. I don't know why. Maybe he was worried I'd advise Laren to leave him. I wouldn't. Not my place. But I couldn't imagine why she'd stay. Not with him gambling away their money every time they have any.

Their horses were already packed with all their gear, and I

noticed they'd hired a fifth horse, for me. Not so fine a steed as the other four, but I knew Dandelion, and she was a good mare. Three years old, and had a gentle disposition if you didn't mistreat her. Always liked her coat, too. Sort of a soft gray, with a streak of white running down between her eyes. Like a streak of mischief.

Her packs were mostly full of gear and food, but there was still room for my pack of clothes.

I almost thought we were ready to go, but as soon as we saddled up, Edan turned to me and asked, "Which smith do you consider the town's finest?"

"Bolan," I answered readily enough.

"Who's the second best?" Duron asked. "No reason to pay top—"

Ig snorted. "Only a damned fool stints on arms or armor. Bolan it is."

"This from the one who hates paying for tea."

"It's *leaves*. You're paying for hot water and *leaves*. Just dunk some grass in the river, while you're at it."

Duron turned to Qala for support. "What do you say?"

"I say I like tea. And if I have to be up before the sky blues, I'll damn well have it."

"I mean about the armor."

Qala's turn to snort. "Zian here is a lot finer to look at than those books you love so much, Duron. And I won't have him getting killed because you were too cheap to buy him decent armor. Bolan it is."

I gave her a grateful smile then, and the wink she gave me that time had more oomph to it.

I wasn't sure Bolan kept any kind of stock of armor and weapons, but apparently there was enough call for him to keep some on hand. And while Ig bartered with him over which armor and weapons, and what they'd pay, I walked over to where Yinda was working, to chat with her.

Her part of the forge was already hot. She was shaping iron that looked to be for bracing the sides of a cart. The strip she worked was long enough that only the part she hammered was orange.

I'd never gotten to see Yinda work before, but her muscles were impressive, going about their task. She kept that hammer going at a good, steady pace. She didn't dress fancy while working, either. Roughspun for both her tunic and breeches, and a leather apron. Her hair was tied back in a knot behind her head.

She paused when she saw me approaching. Frowned like she'd caught me napping when I was supposed to be baling.

"What are you doing here, Zian Sonnalsson?"

"You know the old waterfall cave?"

Yinda didn't answer, except maybe to give me a look that said it was a stupid question and not *worthy* of an answer.

"Well, those four are paying me to take them to it."

She scrunched up her face the way she always did when she got suspicious. Looked over at Bolan and Ig just as Ig was pointing to me.

Soon as the pieces fell into place, her face got hot with anger. "They're buying for *you*."

Didn't say it loud. Just said it like the last word was supposed to puncture my skin.

I nodded, a little embarrassed.

"What do *you* know about wearing armor and swinging weapons, Zian Sonnalsson? Nothing. That's what. And you've got no business pretending otherwise."

"I'm not pretending anything," I snapped back, feeling a little angry now myself. "I don't plan on doing any fighting. But Old Nik always says that's when you're most likely to *need* to fight. And better to be ready than not."

Yinda scoffed and viciously shoved part of the iron she was working into the coals of her furnace.

"So the Purple Gryphon's not exciting enough for you anymore? Got to go get yourself killed, is that it?"

"Stop talking to me like I'm a child. I know the area. I'm a guide. That's all. The armor and weapon, they're just in case something goes wrong in a way they don't expect."

Yinda scoffed again. "Believe that, do you? And they're tossing away good money to get you armor they don't figure you'll need?"

"I told you. Better to—"

"Yeah, yeah. You come back alive, come tell me the story. You don't, well, then I hope Taesark has a soft spot for fools."

Not much I could say to that. If I stood before Taesark at the entrance to the Fields of Narath-Te, then I could only hope the god of judgment took pity on me.

Yinda didn't wait for a reply anyway. Went back to work. And even if I thought of one, I couldn't have used it. Ig called me over for fitting.

For armor, they got me a chain mail shirt that hung down to my wrists and about halfway down my thighs. To go with it, a chain mail coif. For a weapon, Bolan recommended a battle axe.

"I know you've swung an axe plenty," he said to me, "and while this isn't quite the same, it's a lot closer to what you know than a warhammer, maul, or sword."

"What about a spear?" Duron asked.

Bolan shook his head. "We don't hunt boar around here. He'll have no instinct for it, the way he will an axe. He's a good hand with a bow, though."

"We have no need of another archer," Edan said, and Bolan really looked at Edan as though seeing them for the first time. Slowly nodded.

"Right then. Try a few cuts with this."

Bolan tossed me an axe with a big enough haft and head that I needed both hands to hold and swing it with any control. Only one side was bladed, though. On the other side had a spike, big enough to lend some balance to the blade side.

My first cut was down, but Ig laughed and said, "You're not cutting wood with *that*."

"Blow could've cleaved a skull," Bolan said, defending me. "He's right, though. More often you'll want to swing that side to side."

I whipped it around a few times. The weight was fine, and I felt that I had good enough control over where the edge went.

After a few such practice strokes, I nodded at Bolan, who shook his head in wonder.

"You're a far cry from the little lad I used to see running around town, Zian. You take care, now."

"I will," I said, and shook hands with him while Ig paid an assistant.

And then, at last, we were on our way.

I ALMOST FELT GUILTY, TAKING MONEY TO BE A GUIDE, AS WE LEFT THAT day. I mean, the route didn't seem all that complex to me.

First, you have to get past the farms. And yeah, that'll take about half a day.

Quarter of a day, as it turned out, because we started not at a walk, but at a trot. Ig, it seemed, was tired of being surrounded by farmland, and none of the others tried to gainsay him.

For her part, Dandelion seemed happy to stretch her legs, so I didn't raise a fuss either.

Once the farms were behind us, and we slowed our pace, it was mostly valley grass from Terand's Bend to the foothills. There'd be a few groves of nut elms or cankers, but the nut elms weren't close enough to be worth our while. And cankers are useless for shade. Grow straight up, branches and leaves both. Not an inch of spread to those trees.

There'd be more nut elms and some dogwood once we got to the foothills before the start of the mountains, which was where we were going. But I had a hard time imagining anyone getting lost between Terand's Bend and that old waterfall cave, even if they didn't have much more than a decent set of directions.

Tell you, though, any feeling I might've had that I wasn't earning my money, it faded as the sun grew higher.

The day warmed faster than it should've. Seemed we were in for an earlier heat wave than usual. Wasn't sure how to take that, as signs went.

I mean, heat and a clear sky had to be more auspicious than, say, a downpour of rain, a thunderstorm, or an unseasonable snow, right?

But on the other hand, the sun kind of settled into my chain mail, warming it slowly. And that chain mail clutched tightly to every bit of warmth it pulled in.

Meant that by the time we stopped – around midday – I was sweating and more than happy to pull off that coif and a break from that feeling of being slow-cooked. I'd've taken off the chain mail shirt as well, but Ig was still wearing his. And his included leggings. Though he didn't wear a coif. But that was because he had a good, steel helm hanging from his saddlebags.

Anyway, the heat wasn't all I needed a break from, I can tell you.

Up until that day, I'd only ridden a horse a few times in my life. There really just wasn't any need for it. The only times I'd been on horseback were when Kue Rinton bought some new stock, which had happened maybe ... five times since I was big enough to help when she did.

Her stablemaster used me as a "test rider." Figured if a horse would cooperate with me, who just about never even *sat* on one let alone rode it, that horse would cooperate with anyone. And Kue Rinton needed some pliable horses among her stock, to be lent or rented to certain types of moneyed individuals.

Or at least that was as close as I ever got to an explanation.

So a few times in my life, I'd spent an hour or so riding a few different horses around. And apart from two specific horses – and I remembered well that there'd been exactly *two* – who had been far less biddable to an inexperienced rider than the sellers had promised, my experiences had been good, but fairly brief.

Yeah, those were two unfun rides. One of them was on the back of a brown stallion that bolted. All I could do was hold on and wait for him to run himself out. The other one had me riding a blonde mare who treated me well enough – until I tried to ask her to turn.

She immediately bucked and threw me.

Got lucky I didn't break anything. *Was* the first time I ever got knocked out, though.

Woke up surrounded by worried faces, which did more to make me feel better than I would have guessed.

Point is, spending all day in the saddle? Or even half a day, as it had been at that point? Yeah, that was something I wasn't ready for.

I was already sore enough that I felt sure I was walking funny when we took that break. Qala – feeling more like herself by this time, apparently – offered to rub me anyplace that felt sore. But Edan stepped in and instructed me in little ways to change how I sat and how I rode. And made me contort my body in a few ways that Qala described as "very interesting indeed," but did, in fact, help ease a little of my soreness.

Duron had scoffed at the whole issue.

Ig hadn't scoffed, so much, as dismissed the problem. Saying, "Bah! It's good for him. He'll get used to it soon enough."

Edan's pointers helped, though. The second half of the day's ride – while not exactly a *pleasure* – felt better than the morning half had. Leaving the coif in my saddlebag for the second half of the day's ride helped even more.

I figured that if Ig didn't need to wear his helmet yet, I didn't need to wear the coif yet either.

We didn't get as far that day as I'd expected to.

Given that we were on horseback, I'd figured we'd cover the distance faster than I would have hiked it with my friends. But apparently I hadn't appreciated two facts.

First, my friends and I hiked pretty darned fast, when we intended to cover a lot of ground in a single day.

Second, eager as these four adventurers were to get to that cave, apparently they didn't want to get there close to nightfall. They were much happier to walk the horses, take breaks now and again, and camp that night among the nut elms of the foothills, knowing they would reach the cave in the early part of the next morning.

They found a nice grove on a hilltop, with a small clearing in the middle. Just big enough for the five of us to sleep comfortably on the grass, with the horses hobbled nearby.

I started to gather firewood – not that there was much among the nut elms, dogwood was better for firewood – but Ig stopped me.

"No need for that. We won't have a campfire until we're on the way back. No need to draw any attention to ourselves."

"Attention? Who from? There's no one out here, but maybe a couple of hunters. And they'll have their own fires."

"You'd be surprised, my..." He shook his head. "You'd be surprised, Zian."

I did notice he'd been treating me better, since Qala called him out for not using my name.

"We're not hunting elk or mountain goats," Duron said. He still sounded irritable, and he was moving as though his back was stiff.

Mine wasn't so bad. Either Edan's tips were helping, or I was getting used to riding faster than I expected.

But Duron was still talking.

"There are worse things in these hills and mountains than hunting cats. And believe me. You'll want to see them before they see you."

I shook my head and set up my bedroll. I couldn't help but notice that my bedroll ended up near Qala's, but that just looked like chance. Or at least, she wasn't acting like she had any intentions of visiting me in the night.

Of course, I figured out at least part of the reason for that while we sat in the dimming light, gnawing on cold chicken and apples and hunks of a sharp, dried cheese. Just water to drink with that for most of us, though Ig, of course, insisted on his ale.

We'd barely sat down to our repast when Duron said, "No arguments about setting watch, I presume?"

The others all made little sounds that indicated that they were all in agreement about it. Which gave me no information, so I had to ask the question.

"What do you mean?"

"I mean setting watch," Duron said. "What do you think I mean?"

"To set a watch," Edan said in that odd, affectless tone of theirs, "means that while the others sleep, one person remains awake and vigilant for threats. Generally this is done in rotation, so that no one loses too much sleep, or risks becoming inattentive from exhaustion."

"What threats, though?" I shook my head. "Mountain cats aren't likely to come this far out, and nothing else around here is big enough to want to tangle with something our size. We don't look like easy prey."

"It's not the animals we're concerned about," Ig said.

"Other hunters aren't going to tangle with a group like this one either," I said. "I mean it. I've camped out here dozens of times myself, and I know at least thirty others who've done it, just that I could name. Dyaphane's Blood, half of Terand's Bend has camped out here at least once. And I've never heard tell of anyone getting attacked."

"Heard of anyone going missing?" Qala asked, voice just low enough to imply that she knew the answer.

"A couple, yeah. But accidents happen."

"And sometimes, accidents are *made* to happen, Zian," Qala said. "We live the way we do to *keep* 'accidents' from befalling us."

"You guys think something could really happen? Even out here?"

They all nodded grimly. Well, three of them nodded grimly. Edan merely nodded.

"I'll take first watch," Qala said.

"I'll go second," Ig said. "Edan, you want third?"

"I prefer it," Edan said.

"Do you want me to take a watch?" I asked.

"Not what you're paid for," Ig said with a firm shake of his head. "You want to learn, though, I don't mind teaching you. You can join me."

"I'll teach him," Qala said.

Duron snorted, but it was Ig who said, "Not a chance. Need your mind on *what* you're doing, not *who*."

"I beg your pardon," Qala said stiffly. "When have I ever been less than professional, out in the field?"

"Never," Ig said smoothly. "And I don't mean to see you tempted into breaking your record." He turned to me. "You watch with me or you sleep all night. You choose."

"Take the sleep," Duron advised, but he sounded sincere, not surly. "Learn another night. You've had a hard day in the saddle."

"He makes a good point," Ig said. "Sleep tonight, Zian. Learn later."

Qala and Edan both nodded agreement.

Not that I expected sleep to come. I was too sore and too keyed up.

But it came for me all the same.

WHEN I WOKE THE NEXT MORNING, SHORTLY BEFORE DAWN, ONLY EDAN was awake.

"Quietly," Edan said, in a voice that wasn't exactly whispering. It was like he put the same amount of effort into the affectless words, and yet they weren't any louder than a whisper. "Do not wake the others. They will rise on their own soon enough."

"What should I do?" I couldn't match talking the way Edan did, so I settled for whispering.

"Pack, if you can do so quietly. Otherwise, as good for you to lie still. Sleep a little more if you can. Meditate, if you cannot."

"What's 'meditate' mean?"

"Ask me later, when we might speak normally."

I nodded, and settled back down. But once I wake up, I'm up. There's no going back to sleep. So I just lay there as the night sky began to gray.

I smelled the good scents of the nut elms spring. When the nuts just start to bud, they get a smell that reminds me of what they smell like when I roast them. A rich scent. Not strong yet. They were too small. But it was a good, comfortable scent all the same.

I listened to the last of the night birds, finishing up their business for the night. Then the first of the blue tobins began making its three-toned chirps. Blue tobins were small birds, but their chirps sounded like they came from birds two or three times their size.

The chirps of the blue tobin relaxed me that morning. A little bird that could chirp with the bigger birds. And that was kind of what I was doing, after all. Trying to chirp with the four bigger birds around me...

Finally, around the time that the first rays of sunlight began to wake the colors of the world around me, Ig snorted and jerked and jumped to his feet with a wordless shout.

Qala was suddenly out of her bedroll, in a balanced bent-knee crouch. Dagger in each hand, she cast about quickly for threats. She looked like death personified as a beautiful woman.

"Ig," she said, slowly lowering her daggers, "you know I hate when you do that if there's no threat."

"Bah!" Ig said, smiling. "Keeps you sharp. Best way to get up in the morning."

"Speaking of getting up in the morning," Duron said, grouchy as ever. "Better tighten your corset, Qala, or the lad'll pop an eyeball."

"I ... I wasn't..." I said, fumbling for words while Duron's joints popped louder than his words as he stood.

"No?" Qala asked, quirking a half-smile at me. Her hands were empty of daggers again, but I had no idea where she'd put them. Or when she'd done it.

After she held me with that quirked smile for a moment, she winked and said, "Pity."

"Flirt later," Ig said. "We have a long day ahead of us."

Breakfast was little more than day-old bread and water, along with some leftover chicken. Then we were packed, and I had to don that chain mail again. And Ig wore his helmet – like a bowl covering most of his head, and continuing down with a nose guard – so I put the coif on as well.

Edan rode with bow in hand. Qala, I noticed, loosened her sword in its scabbard. Duron checked a few things in the pouches at his belt, mumbling to himself as he did.

I rearranged my pack to make sure I could get to my axe quickly. If I needed it.

My nerves started jangling like the bells on a tinker's cart, and just as discordant. They really were expecting a fight, and sometime soon.

When we saddled up this time, we rode in two ranks. Me and Ig up front, and Qala, Duron and Edan in back.

Ig rode with a lance in hand. I hadn't even realized he'd *had* one. Or, rather, I'd seen it strapped to his horse, but I hadn't realized it was a lance. I'd just thought it was a thick pole. But it had a wicked looking blade at the end.

I led us out of the clearing and through the grassy foothills. The mountainsides nearest us were green with conifers, nut elms, dogwoods and ash trees, along with all kinds of underbrush. But the area I was heading for, a little farther east, was rockier. Dustier. Like when the river course changed, the old course just gave up and died of heartbreak.

The waterfall had been in a small chasm. Part of the reason I'd felt a guide was overkill, really. I mean, when most of the lower mountainside is green and lush, finding the rocky chasm feels like a simple task.

No sense in pointing that out, though. And to be fair, the farther east you go among these mountains, between here and the new river course, at least, is a lot of rocky area.

We kept the horses to something less than a trot. Maybe a quicker kind of walk.

When we reached the edge of the chasm, Ig stopped us. Turned to me.

"How far in is our destination?"

"Not far. A few hundred strides. No more."

Ig nodded. "Qala."

"Agreed," she said, dismounting in a smooth motion and handing her reins to Duron.

Qala began looking around as she approached the chasm mouth. She pointed up and to the left, then made a fist with that hand. Pointed again, higher up and nearly straight ahead, but still a little left. Hesitated. Made a fist.

As her eyes scanned the right side, she only pointed once, but once more she made a fist.

Before I could ask Ig, he told me, in hushed tones.

"She's spotted three likely vantage points where someone could be on lookout. Each of them currently empty, which is good news for us."

I wanted to ask who they expected to be watching, but figured the answer would just be cryptic. They had their system, and they were going to follow it. No matter *how* safe Zian and his friends had *always* been here.

Qala was moving forward on foot now. Slowly. Inspecting the grounds and the chasm walls, and taking long enough that I noticed that the day was already heating up again. It would be another hot one. Even the dust was smelling warmer already.

Qala crouched in the middle of the chasm floor, almost in the exact middle of the chasm walls. She dug into a pouch at her belt and pulled out a small tool of some kind. I couldn't see it in detail. What I could see looked like a small rod of black metal.

She worked at it for a moment, then nodded. She stood, checked again for a few paces, then returned to the group.

"They had a pressure trap. Nothing immediately dangerous. Just a kind of alert system. I think it's tied to some of the looser rocks, so they'd fall when it was tripped. Make enough noise to make sure they knew someone was coming."

"Wouldn't that be kind of obvious?" Ig asked.

"Not the way they did it," Qala said. "Wouldn't feel like more than a little shift in the rock under a hoof or boot. And the rocks that it triggered would be far enough away not to make the trespasser see the connection."

I didn't say anything, but I had to admit. I'd noticed in the past that sometimes the rocky floor of the chasm didn't feel as stable as I'd thought it would be...

"Should be safe to proceed now," she said, and mounted her horse once more.

"All right, guide," Ig said with a small smile. "Onward."

WE REACHED THE OLD WATERFALL SPOT. OVERHANGING ROCKS, smoothed by centuries of water now starting to get rough with regular exposure to wind and grit, snow and rain and sun. And under the overhang, that deep indentation in the cavern wall that my friends and I had promoted to calling a "cave."

Wasn't deep enough for the five of us to camp in – at least, not with the horses – and have us all inside the indentation.

The size of it didn't matter though. Because we had yet to dismount when Ig thumped his fist on his chest. In quiet tones, he said, "What did I tell you? The right kind of rock. That's bachite."

I thought it just looked like granite. Same as most of the rock around us. But then, I'd never heard of bachite before.

We dismounted, but we didn't hobble the horses. Instead, the horses were gathered noses-in, and all of the reins were handed to me. I was to remain near the mouth of the "cave" while the others checked out the "cave walls."

Ig led this. He pulled their map back out, mumbled as he read over the writing, then nodded to himself and handed the map to Duron.

He tried to anyway. Duron wouldn't take it. Shook his head.

"Hasn't changed since I last read it. Should be ten hands left of center, and fifteen hands high. If this is the right place."

"It's the right place," Qala said. "Otherwise, why set that alarm trap?"

"Coincidence?" Duron suggested.

"If so, we will find something at least," Edan said. "If not what we seek."

While they discussed the possibilities at little more than a whisper, Ig gauged the center of the indentation, then counted out the space to the left, then up from the ground. Which put it at just about eye height to him.

"Got it," he said, and the discussion behind him stopped. "Where will it open?"

"It doesn't say that," Duron said, sounding irritated about it. As though he'd like to slap whoever drew that map. Which I could understand, given its inaccuracy. Unless the inaccuracy was intended as some kind of feint...

"Wait," I said, trying for both quiet and intent.

They all looked at me.

"What if it wasn't an accident that the map was off?"

"Even mapmakers make mistakes," Edan said. "Especially if they feel rushed."

"Hold on," Duron said, frowning. "Zian may have a point. The scale of the map might have been a hint that the directions to finding the door's opening were a blind."

"But why would it be?" Ig asked.

"There's no harm in finding out," Qala said, looking contemplative. "All right, Zian. If the mistakes in the map weren't mistakes, what do you think they're trying to tell us?"

"Maybe," I said, but I had to swallow, my mouth was so dry. And my heart was pounding. These people were professionals. Who was I to tell them their business. And yet, I'd come this far...

"Maybe the real opening for the door is proportionally in the same place as the old falls is, compared to the new falls."

"And where do you think that would be?"

"Let me look at the map," Duron said.

"No," Qala said. "Zian spotted the mistakes in the scale. Which means he's the most likely of us to understand the scale quickly."

"I know how to read a map," Duron said drily.

"Let him try," Edan said, and Ig nodded agreement.

"May I see the map again?" I asked, handing the reins to Edan as I stepped closer.

Ig handed me the map. I tried gauging the part where I knew the scale was right against the part where I knew the scale was wrong. Figured out from there, the proportional distance to the site of the old falls.

Then, with a deep breath, I asked Ig to show me where the center bottom of the indentation was, followed by the spot he'd found for the entrance. He went right to both spots, as though he'd memorized them.

"...and the little trigger is right here," Ig finished, showing me the spot he'd been about to push when I stopped him.

I nodded. Fought to steady my breathing while I did math in my head. I moved to a spot five more handspans left, and down three.

I checked myself three times, then nodded. "Should be right about here."

"Should be?" Duron scoffed.

Ig came closer. Studied the rock there. Broke into a laugh.

"Brilliant!" he said, and clapped me on the shoulder. "He's right. There's another tiny panel right where he said there should be. This works, Zian, and there's a bonus in it for you."

My nerves were still kicking up a racket, but I managed a shaky smile.

"Back away now," Ig said. "You want me opening this door. We don't know what's behind it."

I returned to the horses, getting a smile from Qala on my way. When Edan returned the reins to me, they gave me a nod of approval.

I'd won some measure of respect from them in that moment. Even Duron gave me a nod, albeit a little more grudgingly.

But Edan didn't immediately resume their place. First, they handed me my battle axe.

"You might need this," they said softly. "Do not be a hero. Hold back. Protect the horses and yourself."

Well. That feeling of accomplishment blew away like dandelion seeds. My nerves were back, and ringing alarm bells. I suddenly wanted to empty my bladder, and my heart was pounding and my muscles were getting twitchy.

Ig pressed the tiny panel forward until it clicked. That click was a soft sound. No louder than the sound of a tankard being set down on a bar. And yet I heard it, because the rest of them had grown still.

Edan with bow in hand and an arrow nocked. Qala with her sword in hand.

Her sword wasn't like others I'd seen. It was longer, and thinner, with a slight curve and only a single edge.

The click was followed by a low, rumbling sound.

A crack appeared in the center of the indentation, running from the chasm floor to maybe as high as I could reach straight up.

The rumble continued, and like two arched doors, two slabs of rock – bachite, I guess – opened inward. Kicking up dry dust as they did.

On the one hand, this was exciting. Easily the most exciting moment of my life to that point. And I'd helped make it possible.

But on the other hand, I couldn't help thinking about something.

Qala had said that someone had set an alert that involved falling rocks to make noise.

But that rumbling sound had to have carried a pretty fair distance. And likely, whoever set that alert would know what that sound meant.

Whoever my group didn't want to alert now likely knew we were here.

From where I stood, I couldn't see very far inside the newly opened doors in the "cave" under where the old waterfall was. It was pitch black inside, and the dust that had been raised by the opening doors itched at my nose and made me contort my face with the need to sneeze.

I didn't want to sneeze. That just seemed like the worst thing I could possibly—

Okay, fine. I sneezed.

I sneezed so loud it echoed off the cavern walls. As though a thousand little Zians were passing the sneeze somewhere down a very long line.

"In! Now!" Ig barked, and Edan dropped back to take the rear and usher me and the horses in front of them. All the while, keeping a sharp-eyed lookout for trouble behind us with an arrow nocked.

I hustled the horses into what I could now see was a corridor of some sort. Ceiling higher in here. At least twice my height. And the corridor was wider than the doorway, so that all five horses could stand side by side in relative comfort.

I hadn't figured out where the light was coming from – my attention was on the horses while I was struggling to keep my battle axe ready.

But Edan must've done something, because the doors started rumbling closed again, and they were moving past me to rejoin the others.

The doors boomed closed.

"Well," Duron said drily, "safe to say they know we're here now."

"Yes," Ig said, "but if we're lucky they don't know where *here* is. Look how dusty this place is."

And Ig had a point, there seemed to be almost as much air to the air as, well, *air*.

Once I had the horses reasonably calm, I turned around to see if I could spot where that light—

Oh. Of course. Duron was a wizard.

It was like Duron was holding a torch over his head, but he didn't have a torch. The flame just floated there, burning soundlessly but flickering like real fire.

Qala was closely inspecting the floor and walls. Ig was mumbling to himself as he looked past her down the corridor, as though he could see into the darkness beyond where Duron's light could reach.

Edan had their head cocked to one side. Listening, maybe, though what to I couldn't tell. I couldn't hear much beyond the Ig's mumbling, the creak of Qala's leather, and the pounding of my own heart.

"Looks good," Qala said, returning. "That sneeze aside, all this dust is a blessing. Easier to check dusty surfaces. We should be able to make reasonably good time."

"What about him?" Duron said, jerking his head to indicate me.

"Wasn't his fault he sneezed," Ig said. "Not used to it like we are, and none of us warned him."

"I don't mean *that*," Duron said with forced patience. "I mean the obvious thing. We're all in agreement, yes? That he remain here with the horses, the way he was *supposed* to remain *outside*, with the horses?"

Qala frowned, but it was Edan who spoke.

"Better that he accompany us now."

"And if someone else comes through the door, they just get free horses and supplies, do they?"

"Ig's right," Qala said. "No one's been down this corridor in hundreds of years. Safe to say the local threats don't know how to open these doors. If they even know the doors are there. Which they might not."

"We can hobble the horses," Ig said. "And they'll be just fine here in the dark. I'm thinking Zian deserves a chance to come with us."

"I agree," Qala said.

"Of course you do," Duron grumbled.

"Not because I like the way he looks," Qala said, irritated. "Because he's already proven he's clever and strong. We might just find we need him."

"*Need* is a strong word," Duron said.

"Would benefit from his presence then," Edan said. "Either way, the majority is against you here, Duron. Zian is coming."

"Does he even want to?" Duron asked.

"More than a little rude," Ig said, "asking us that question and not him." Ig nodded at me. "What do you say, Zian? Care to trod some rock that no one's walked in hundreds of years? See a few things you'll never see, back at the Purple Gryphon?"

It was a terrifying thought, in some ways. But the answer jumped out of me all the same.

"Absolutely."

"Well if you *phrase* it that way, of course he wants to come," Duron said, then turned to me, his eyes burning with inner light. "Which would you rather do, Zian? Remain here in safety, doing something you know how to do, tend animals? Or would you rather risk your young life and come with us? Facing threats the like of which even *we* may never have seen before. Knowing your life might be snuffed out without warning, in darkness, by some unspotted trap or deadfall. By a sudden struggle with some fantastical enemy whose mere presence makes you douse your breeches."

"Sounds terrifying," I said.

"It will be," Duron said with a nod and an air of satisfaction.

"Well," I said, taking a deep breath, "Dad always said I had to face my fears or they'd shrink me smaller than a blade of grass. I guess I'd better come."

"Ha!" Qala said with a smirk. "Well said."

"You're not listening, boy," Duron said, stepping closer. "I'm not talking about some fear of heights, or—"

"You're talking about the worst kind of fear," I said. "The unknown. And when will I get a better chance to face it? Or better company when I do?"

Ig chuckled, and said to Qala, "I'm starting to like this one." To me and Duron, he said, "It's settled then. Zian comes with us."

Ig then stepped in close to Duron. Even though he had to look at him, the shorter man still gave a sense of looming. "And you should stop calling him boy. He's proven more than once that he's a man."

I'D SPENT MOST OF MY LIFE INDOORS, TO THAT POINT, AND A reasonable amount of it underground. In the little warren of rooms and halls and cellars underneath the Purple Gryphon.

But walking down that dusty corridor with those four adventurers, that was something else entirely.

The dust didn't smell like normal dust. It had this ... weight of age to its odor. Something in the dryness of it, maybe. Beyond that, I couldn't quite put my finger on it.

And speaking of weight, I slowly became very aware of the tons of rock overhead. As we moved down that first corridor, we were leaving the chasm behind, which meant, little by little, we were putting a *whole mountain* above us.

It wasn't thoughts of that that made me shiver, though. At least, I didn't think that was it. I'm pretty sure it was the chill to the air in there. Much colder than that unseasonable heat that most of the valley would be suffering through that day. The horses were probably glad to be inside.

I held my battle axe in both hands, but had to keep shifting my grip because of the sweat on my palms.

My words might've been brave before – and Dad really did say that about facing fears – but no denying that what Duron said had gotten to me. Even though I was walking at the back of the group, I kept expecting the floor beneath me to give out. Or maybe an arrow to spring forth out of the wall.

Or worst of all, maybe some dreadful noragh or plisk would stalk out of the legends and murder me from behind, taking my body back to feast upon. Or worse, lay eggs in…

Not thoughts that were helping, but they did ensure that I didn't lag behind the group.

Not that we were moving very fast.

Qala led the way, sword in hand. Watching the walls, floor and ceiling more than she watched the corridor ahead of her.

Ig followed a few steps behind, warhammer in one hand and battle axe in the other, but his attention was down the corridor past Qala.

Duron followed a few steps behind Ig. He had one hand raised and gesturing like a steward instructing workers. And with each gesture, his floating fire moved about so that it aided Qala's search for hazards.

Edan walked last except for me. Bow in hand, but all arrows in their quiver, which they wore strapped low along the right thigh, near their free hand.

I kept glancing over my shoulder. Expecting something to sneak up on us, even though I knew nothing was there. I just couldn't help it. The horses were somewhere behind me in the darkness. I knew that. And they hadn't made any distressed sounds. I knew that too.

But I kept feeling this … creeping sensation along the back of my neck. Like maybe something was following us, and I just couldn't spot it. Maybe it had hid when we passed, now trailed us. Lurking just beyond our light.

Watching. Waiting.

I tried to shove that feeling aside. To keep my focus on where we were and what we were doing. But, well, all I was really doing was walking.

I mean, yes, I was wearing all that chain mail and I was carrying a battle axe, but it wasn't like I knew what I was doing with either of them. The others all had some idea of where they should be looking, and for what, and what they should be doing while they walked.

I was just ... walking. And trying to be "ready." Though ready for what, I couldn't begin to guess.

Also, maybe it was my imagination, but I thought the floor was sloping. Like each step forward was slightly lower than the step before it. I thought about saying something about this, but the others all had to know that, right? I mean, this was what they *did*. Surely if I could notice a thing like that, they had to have noticed it first. And probably knew what it meant. And adjusted their plans accordingly.

All without having to say a word about it, because they had experience at this stuff, and I didn't.

I was just starting to think I'd made a mistake in coming. Not in leaving the Purple Gryphon in the first place, but in leaving the horses. Back there with the horses, I would've known what to do. But down here? Doing what people called "adventuring?"

I'd probably be more trouble than I was worth. I'd probably—

Qala halted the group by showing us her palm, fingers stiff and together. She was facing the left side of the rocky corridor, which looked just the same to me as the rest of this rocky corridor.

"There's something here," she said. "And unless I'm mistaken" – she pointed to several spots with her sword – "I'm picking out the outline of a door."

"The text said nothing about hidden doors or side ventures," Duron said. "I say we pass it by for now and check it on the way out."

"The text said nothing about old and new waterfalls, nor about tests in its guidance," Edan said. "If we do not investigate this, we may miss the object of our quest entirely. Better that we check it now."

I wanted to ask then just what the object of this quest was, but it didn't seem the time.

"I think we all know I want to open it," Qala said with a quirked smile. "Ig?"

"Tell me again what the text tells us?" Ig asked.

Duron, to my surprise, answered straight and without the slightest sign of irritation or grouchiness to his voice.

"'Folly lies in the depths. Blessed is the snake's tongue, but cursed the tines of the hayfork. Death awaits you, but victory lies beyond it.'"

"Right, right," Ig said. "Folly lies in the depths, so we shouldn't go too deep."

"But we're descending with every step down the corridor," I said without thinking.

They all looked at me. Duron and Ig looked surprised, and Ig and Qala looked pleased. Edan merely looked.

"Right you are," Ig said, giving me a smile. "We've been descending slowly for the last four hundred feet."

How he could have known that so precisely, I had no idea. But the others all took that as a statement of fact. Even Duron.

"Point is," Ig continued, addressing the group now, "we should at least open the door and see where it leads. If it's a faster route leading deeper under the mountain, then it's the wrong way for us."

"What does the rest of the riddle mean?" I asked.

Duron scoffed, but Qala said, "There's no reason not to tell him."

She nodded at Ig.

"The part of the text that Duron quoted deals with directions. The language is a bit ... overwrought to my way of thinking—"

"It's clear enough," Duron said.

"—but what it *means*," Ig continued, "is clear enough. The snake's tongue has two prongs. So when we come to a fork in the path, we take the blessed route. Which is..."

"He's an apprentice then, is he?" Duron grumbled.

"Ignore him," Qala said. "They worship Urtrens the Holy in Terand's Bend, don't they?"

I nodded. Urtrens was easily the most popular god anywhere farmers were numerous. Urtrens' priests gave the best blessings to crops and fields and livestock, so long as the proper sacrifices were made. And those sacrifices weren't too dear, as gods went.

"Well, this mapmaker was from a place where Urtrens was worshiped," Qala said. "So if the snake's tongue is a fork in the road, what does blessing it mean?"

"'The left hand path is the path of the righteous,'" I quoted. That was the reason that fields were always sewn and harvested right to left. Even writing was done from right to left, so that one's words remained on the path of righteousness in the eyes of Urtrens. "So we turn left."

"Very good," Ig said. "Care to hazard a guess about the rest of it?"

"A hayfork has three tines," I said. "If the left hand path is the path of the righteous, then the right hand path is the path of the curséd blasphemer. And if the hayfork is cursed, then we take a right the first time we have three choices?"

"Wonderful," Duron grumbled. "We've proven he knows his left from his right. Can we proceed?"

"Certainly," Qala said, turning back to what still looked to me like a bare patch of rock. A dagger showed up in her off-hand – I swear, I didn't see her draw it – and she began tapping here and there with the pommel.

I drew ... maybe a dozen breaths while she conducted her search before she said, "Ha! Ready?"

Edan nocked an arrow. Ig raised his weapons. I raised my battle axe in hands shaky with a need to fight or run. My body would have been happy with either. Possibly even happier with running.

Qala, her knife gone and her sword raised, did something along the rockface, and a section of the wall just slid to the side.

Quietly. Quieter than a well-oiled door. Quieter than a stalking cat, even.

On the other side, another corridor. Narrower. I could almost touch both sides at the same time. No shorter though.

And it sloped away sharply.

"Looks like a quick descent," Ig said with a sigh.

"That is a deception," Edan said. "This is our snake's tongue, and before us lies the blessed prong of that tongue."

"Most people don't think of side doors the way they think of branching passages in a corridor," Qala said suspiciously.

"True," Duron said with a sigh, "but that interpretation is consistent with all the other slightly off directions we've gotten so far. This is probably our left."

"Seems a bit sharp a descent though," Ig said. "I agree we should check it, but we should establish how far down we're willing to go before we decide we've chosen the wrong path."

"Is 'depths' a general word, like 'people?'" I asked. "Or a specific word, like 'Bendsfolk?'"

"It's..." Ig frowned, then chuckled. "It gets used both ways a lot. But when it's specific, and dealing with a mountain, 'depths' refers to the heart under the mountain."

They all looked at each other like Ig had just made some big revelation that I didn't get.

"So ... that word is important?"

"Given the way dear old Great Uncle Egrun wrote the rest of this portion of the text," Duron said with a sigh, "it is."

"Your great uncle?"

"Technically, about four generations back," Duron said, "but yes, one of my forebears. And given his word games so far, we'd best assume he meant 'depths' specifically, not generally."

"Which suggests that it isn't a downward slope we should avoid," Edan said, "but a course that would lead us to the heart under the mountain."

"The blessed path it is," Ig said, gesturing for Qala to begin checking the new passage.

THE SIDE PASSAGE WASN'T AS DUSTY AS THE MAIN PASSAGE, WHICH seemed to bother the others, so it bothered me. Of course, they didn't say *why* it bothered them, so I think I just assumed that it meant that while centuries might have passed since anyone last went down the *main* corridor behind the indentation in the chasm where once that waterfall fell, *this* part of what I assumed was a network of corridors was *occupied*.

A thought that made me wonder about these corridors. Because they *were* corridors. Squared off and cut out of the rockface with such precision that they didn't appear to need buttressing.

I'd heard about mines, from the occasional miners that came through the Purple Gryphon. And they made their mines sound a lot more primitive than what we were walking through. I'd gotten the impression that mines weren't anybody's idea of squared off, and that they needed frequent buttressing. And that cave-ins were still an issue, despite their best efforts.

And yet, here I was. I'd come hundreds, maybe more than a thousand feet down a squared off corridor that looked as strong as any of the halls under the Purple Gryphon. Stronger even, because the underside of the Purple Gryphon had supports here and there.

Who dug this out? Squared it off? Given the corners those sharp, precise angles? When had they done it? And what had happened to them?

Things to ponder as we continued along.

The new passage had a slightly wet smell to the air. A fetid kind of wet smell, which I didn't like at all.

My stomach didn't like it either. It had been pestering me for some time now that we had to have passed the point where civilized people stopped for lunch. But once that wet, fetid smell hit my nostrils and tongue, my stomach shut right up.

If anything, my belly gained a touch of queasiness, suggesting that food would be a *bad* idea now. Gave me a bad taste in my mouth. Like my stomach was considering ... a more active protest, but not at that point yet.

Either way, the odor didn't seem to bother the others, as we made our slow way down the sharper slope of that side passage by the light of Duron's floating fire.

It wasn't the slope that slowed us down. It was Qala. Since there wasn't so much dust, she needed longer to check the floor and walls ahead of us. And three or four times she stopped, pulled some small bit of metal from a pouch at her belt, and fiddled with something on the floor or wall before nodding that it was safe to proceed.

I wasn't sure I knew what it was she was doing, but I definitely knew I didn't want to ask. I mean, it was a safe bet that whatever she did protected us from one kind of threat or other. And I had a feeling that the details would just make that creeping sensation along the back of my neck get worse.

It was still there, by the way. That creeping sensation. I'd expected that maybe I'd lose it when we left that main corridor. But no, it followed me down that side passage, behind the hidden door. If anything, the sensation might've gotten worse, because we didn't close the door behind us.

It was Ig's words that made that call, though the others agreed. He'd said, "Better to not have it in our way, if we have to leave in a hurry."

A notion that didn't exactly do anything to ease my worries. If anything, it made me glance over my shoulder even more often. Not that I saw, or heard, anything except the stretch of corridor I'd just crossed. Looking and acting just as unoccupied as it had been when I was crossing it, before fading into darkness at the edge of our light.

That side corridor did eventually curve to the left and level off, which the others took as a good sign. Presumably it indicated that we were moving away from the heart under the mountain.

To be honest, I couldn't have told you which direction we were facing if you gave me two guesses and a clue.

Not long after the corridor leveled off, we came to what the others immediately pronounced a "hayfork." Which, as a former famer, rankled me more than a little.

You see, the corridor ahead of us split four ways. Two of the splits were perfectly squared off left and right turns. The other two – one left and one right – were about evenly spaced between the hard turns.

And four tines was too many for a proper hayfork.

"Zian," Duron said, and when I looked at him, he continued. "Check me on this. Urtrens spoke of the right-hand path and left-hand path, not the hard right, the gentle right, the gentle left and the hard left. Correct?"

"I'm not a priest," I said, hesitantly, "so I don't know *all* the writings and parables. But I only ever heard people talk about the path of the righteous – the left hand path – and the path of the blasphemer – the right hand path. I don't know of any ... refinements to the idea."

"That suggests," Duron said slowly, "that we take the hard right. Because it's got to be the most cursed, yes?"

"But the quote said that cursed are the 'tines' of the hayfork," Qala said. "Plural."

"No verb in that part of the sentence," Duron said, but not as though he was contradicting her. More that he was adding a point of information. "Probably for that reason. To create confusion between the singular verb and plural noun."

"Wait," Edan said, turning to me. "Zian. Earlier you said that a hayfork has *three* tines. But I have seen hayforks made with two tines, or four. Why did you specify three?"

"A proper hayfork has two or three tines," I said. "Two is ... all right, I suppose, but I personal consider three optimal, in terms of strength and utility. And it's one of the few points I agree on with my father *and* my brother."

"What about four?" Qala asked.

"At four tines..." I shook my head. "At four you're either adding weight that you'll regret the first time you spend a morning moving hay or grains with it. If you aren't adding that weight, you have to thin all four tines to keep the same weight as a two or three tine. Which means your new hayfork might not last a whole season without needing to be straightened once or twice."

"Which would weaken it," Ig said, nodding.

"And it won't last as long," I said. "Might even break, if you like each forkful on the heavy side."

"This raises a question," Edan said, without telling me what the question was. Which, to be honest, I found more irritating than their complete lack of intonation while speaking. *That* I'd gotten used to faster than I'd expected.

"Are all four of these branches legitimate options," Duron said, not making it sound like a question, even though I was pretty sure he meant that as the question Edan had just referred to.

Honestly, keeping up with half-conversations like this wasn't easy. And it seemed sometimes that half a conversation was all these four had bothered with since we left the horses. Implying far more than they actually gave voice to.

"Well," Qala said with a deep breath, "guess figuring that out is my job."

"Wait," Duron said, raising one hand, his face set in what I thought was concentration. "Let me have a look first."

She gestured for him to help himself.

From a pouch at his belt, Duron pulled out a piece of charcoal. Staring at the floor, he said, "Center?"

"Exact center is two paces in front of you," Ig said, "and a half-pace left."

"Thank you," Duron said, taking those steps so that he now stood in the exact center of the intersection. He paused for a moment – likely in case Ig offered a correction – then took a half-step back, knelt and in the exact center sketched some kind of sigil on the stone with his charcoal, while mumbling something that sounded like it might've been words, but if so, I had no idea what language it was.

Around the sigil, he sketched a series of progressively larger geometric shapes. A triangle first, then a square, then a series of more triangles.

Took me a moment to figure it out, but I realized that each triangle outside the square had one point pointing back the way we'd come, while the other two varied. Each time, the other two points indicated some combination of the four branching corridors.

He had to slowly move around the sigil to do this, as the shapes kept getting larger and larger. Eventually the rest of us had to move back to give him room.

Largest of all was a pentagon whose each point indicated a different branch.

Just inside and outside each point of that pentacle, Duron sketched the same squiggly sigil he'd started with.

"Guard me please," Duron said without looking up from the rocky floor.

Edan nocked an arrow and raised the bow to a ready position. Ig raised his weapons and accompanied Duron as he moved to the mouth of each of the five corridors – including the one we'd come down to get here, which would have been the shaft of the hayfork.

On the floor just inside each mouth, Duron sketched that sigil again.

Finally, he returned to the center of the intersection and checked his handiwork. Nodded to himself.

He put away his charcoal and, from another pouch at his belt, pulled a fistful of something. He held up his hand and opened it, palm up, showing that he held some quantity of a reddish powder.

He tossed the powder into the air and snapped out a word I didn't catch.

With a sweet smell of stargazer blossoms, the powder flared into velvety crimson brilliance. First as a blazing ball, but the ball resolved into a sigil – the same sigil Duron had been sketching.

Tendrils lanced out from the sigil and struck each other depiction of that sigil at the same time. Both those in the center of the intersection and those in the mouth of each branch of the corridor.

At each place, the charcoal burned an even brighter red. So bright I winced away from it. A wave of pale, pinkish smoke rolled up from the floor, filling the intersection for a moment, before dispersing.

All on its own. It didn't spread out first, or rise, or fall. It just filled the air around us, then faded like daylight in a forest at dusk.

Once I could see again, I saw that there'd been a change.

The hard right corridor was no longer a corridor. It was now a yawning drop off into inky blackness, about fifteen feet in.

"Illusion," Duron said, shaking his head. "Always hated that kind of magic. Never made any sense to me."

"Least you can break it," Ig said, clapping him on the shoulder while I tried to make sense of what they were saying.

That right-most branching corridor had been faked by magic? It had *always* been nothing more than a vicious drop off that had just *looked* like a real corridor?

I swallowed hard, and my stomach threatened to bring back whatever it was still working on of that morning hard bread.

That was a far cry from the kind of little illusions I'd seen in the Purple Gryphon, cast by wizards to go along with stories they told each other.

Qala moved over to inspect the mouth of that ... or rather of what *had been* a corridor. She shook her head. Pointed to the fifteen feet of corridor that was still there.

"All that's on a lever trigger. Soon as it holds enough weight, it'll fall away like a broken branch, then spring back into place."

"Definitely the most cursed tine," Duron said with a nod. "But not the one that we wanted."

Duron gave me a smile then. First smile I'd ever seen on his face, and I have to admit I found it a little disquieting. He was always just so cantankerous. But right then, I'd swear he was trying to be reassuring.

"Looks as though my Great Uncle Egrun agreed with your family about hayforks." He nodded to the drop off. "That fourth tine just broke right off."

To my frank disbelief, I found myself smiling back at him.

<hr>

By this point, I was glad I'd decided not to wait back with the horses. Yeah, my nerves were jumpy and my palms were sweaty and my stomach was still threatening to bring up whatever it had available.

But I also couldn't deny a few things.

I'd helped find a hidden door that led to a corridor where *no one had walked in centuries*. And what a corridor! Cut right out of the mountain stone with what looked to me like perfect right angles. Smooth walls and flooring.

Yeah, they hadn't needed me to find the hidden door that had led to the side passage we'd been following. But my knowledge of hayforks – and maybe the ways of Urtrens the Holy – might just have saved all four of them from tumbling to their deaths down that corridor that was just an illusion and a drop-off.

All right. These guys were clearly experienced enough at what they did that the probably wouldn't have died there. But I was pretty sure I'd helped, at least a little.

And so far, scary as it had been, I hadn't been in any real danger. Or at least, I'd never *felt* as though I had. I mean, I still wasn't sure what Qala had done with those little tools of hers whenever she'd stopped our progress to do something. But I was pretty sure she was preventing something bad from happening to us.

Yeah, the wet, fetid smell to the air was getting stronger, once we started following "the cursed tine of the hayfork." That is, the right-most *actual* corridor from that branching intersection.

It curved around to the right after a little ways, then led to a set of stairs that looked just as precisely cut as everything else did down here.

"Can't fault their craftsmanship," I said, which got a laugh and a shoulder-clap out of Ig, as though I'd made some kind of joke.

In fact, the others were smiling too – well, Edan wasn't, but Duron and Qala both were – as though they, too, were in on a joke I hadn't tried to tell.

The stairs went up. And we took them the same way we'd taken everything else so far.

Qala in front, checking every step of the way, both walls and stairs.

Ig next, battle axe and warhammer ready in his hands, as he watched the stairs ahead of Qala.

Duron next, directing his floating flame where it would most help Qala with her checking.

Edan last of the four, bow in hand a free hand down near their quiver.

I followed last. Still checking over my shoulder every few steps, because I still couldn't shake that feeling that something was trailing us, just beyond our light.

Couldn't see anything but what we'd just crossed. Couldn't hear anything but our movement and my own nervous heartbeat. And yet, I was sure something was there.

In fact, we'd gone maybe a hundred steps up when I said, voice low, "Hang on a second."

Edan whirled, nocking an arrow and checking the stairs behind me. All three of the others looked back, as though expecting attack from behind.

"I..." My face got hot and my heart pounded harder. "It's probably nothing."

"What is probably nothing?" Edan said, eyes still scanning the fading light back down the stairs.

"I ... it's just..."

"Go ahead, Zian," Qala said. "Tell us."

"I keep getting this feeling like we're being followed. I can't see or hear anything, but—"

"Creeping sensation?" Duron asked, voice tight and alert. "Back of the neck?"

"Yes."

"Smell anything odd?"

"Just that wet, fetid smell."

Ig and Qala rushed down to me, weapons ready.

"How strong?" Qala said.

"How long have you smelled it?" Ig asked.

The both sounded so urgent I started hyperventilating. They were sniffing the air and looking around, but it was Duron who came up to me. Gave me a firm slap that stopped the hyperventilating.

"Answer them," he said simply, but his eyes were studying me sharply.

"Um, pretty strong I guess. First noticed it once we started down the path of the righteous."

"That long?" Ig said and shook his head. "Should've spoken up before."

He started waving his weapons around in the air as though expecting to find something.

Meanwhile, Duron mumbled words I didn't catch. Pulled out his charcoal and traced a symbol on my forehead.

He smacked the symbol with his palm and barked a word in my face.

"Augh!" I shouted, as the back of my neck burned, swift and sudden and gone as fast as it started.

"There!" Duron said, pointing back past me.

I whirled around, battle axe all but forgotten in my one hand and my other hand clutching the sore back of my neck. I suddenly felt both famished and exhausted, and I didn't smell that fetid smell anymore.

What I saw when I looked back though was...

I didn't know what it was.

It had six short legs, each a uniform thickness – about as thick as my thighs – from the hip to the ... feet? I think there were toes at the bottom of those legs.

Its skin was a sickly, mottled green color. Its body was thick as a prized sow, but its head was blunted. Sloping. With an angular mouth full of sharp teeth, and three and a half tentacles stretching out from it. That half-tentacle flailed as though in pain, and looked burnt...

Qala was dancing close to the front, cutting at the tentacles with her sword. Edan started putting arrows into the thing.

Ig bellowed and charged, swinging both his warhammer and his battle axe at the thick hide of the beast. His blade bit, but not deep.

Barely enough to open the surface. Though his hammer thumped hard against it.

Edan's arrows stuck in the creature, but hardly any brackish blood dripped from where they hit. And Qala was nipping bits off the tentacles, but not doing much more than that.

Something clicked inside me.

That burnt tentacle. It had been attached to me. This *thing* had been attached to *me*. *Feeding* on me maybe.

I felt repulsed. But with that repulsion came a spike of adrenaline.

I went with that spike. With a roar of my own, I charged the free side of the thing, chopping down with my battle axe like it was an ironwood stump I needed to split in a single chop.

To my surprise, my axe bit deep. Deep enough that the thing hissed in pain, tentacles retracting.

Ig redoubled his fury, hammer and axe both pummeling far faster than I could even recover to swing a second time. Edan peppered the creature with more arrows, which seemed to sink deeper now. And Qala thrust the tip of her sword down the creature's gullet.

Before much longer, the creature fell dead.

Sadly, even in bloody death, that thing smelled better than what I'd been smelling while it was ... attached ... to me?

I managed to get two stairs up from its corpse before I dropped my weapon and collapsed.

Just like that, Qala was at my side. Touching my face and studying my eyes.

"He'll be fine," Duron said. "But he needs to eat something and sit for a bit. He's young and strong, and we got to him in time. What the kaldip stole, his body will replenish quick enough."

"Might as well all have a break and a snack," Ig said, digging into the pack he wore.

He passed around bits of spiced dried meat for us to chew on, and a skin of water. Ig, of course, kept his own skin for ale.

Qala stayed with me while we rested, checking on me. After we'd been sitting for a few minutes, she said, "Anything else strange happens down here, just say something. Don't worry if you think it's obvious, like a strange odor."

I nodded. "What was that thing?"

"A kaldip. They can walk on walls and ceilings, and if they get a tentacle on you they become all but undetectable, apart from that stench."

"What was..." I swallowed. "What was it doing to me?"

"Sucking out a bit of your life force. Fortunately for you, it was too young to be able to do so very fast."

"Does that mean—"

"That there are others around here?" Ig said. "Probably not. Or at least, not anywhere near us. They're jealous hunters and will fight each other, even if they have enough prey to go around."

"The horses!" I said with a start.

"Are probably fine," Ig said soothingly. "Kaldips don't like the taste of animals."

"Then what was it surviving on down here?"

They all looked at each other.

"Let's just say," Ig said, "we need to keep watch in this area."

"It's good you were able to fight the kaldip," Qala said. "Once they've attached to a victim, they become especially tough to everyone *but* the victim. Would've taken us a lot longer to kill it, if you hadn't hacked into it with your axe."

"It was a good blow," Ig said, smiling.

Duron nodded. Grudgingly said, "Many in your position would've been useless, once they discovered what had been feeding on them. Maybe there was some wisdom in letting you come along."

"Someone should clean the spot where the tentacle touched him," Edan said.

"Not necessary," Duron said. "They don't carry disease. At least, their tentacles don't."

"Better safe than sorry," Qala said. Ig snorted as she dug a small jar of salve out of her belt pouch.

With a rag and some water from a skin, she scrubbed the sore area on the back of my neck. Then she rubbed a little salve into it.

I'd thought that would be the end of it, but no. She blew on the salve for a moment, then washed the area clean one more time.

And I have to admit, it felt better.

Then Qala gave that spot a kiss, and it felt better still. In fact, I now felt ready to continue.

I'd fought my first monster and lived. I was starting to think I'd survive this venture.

AFTER WE RESTED FOR A TIME, WE STARTED UP THE STAIRS AGAIN. We just ... left the corpse of the kaldip on the stairs behind us. Then again, I wasn't sure what else we could do with it. I mean, even if we cut it up, what were we supposed to do? Bring it along? Nothing that smelled that bad could make for good eating. And the hide didn't look like anything I'd want to tan and wear.

I'd lost that feeling of being watched, which was interesting. I mean, I'd had that feeling *before* the kaldip had attached itself to me, as I understood it. That hadn't happened until I smelled that fetid odor.

So some of that feeling of being watched, that had just been ... nerves, I guess? And apparently I'd gotten over those nerves. Because though I still checked behind me every few steps, I didn't feel any urgency about it. More as a matter of course.

Maybe that was even my role in the group, at this point. Rear guard. I felt ready for it, if so. My palms weren't even as sweaty as they had been. I felt more confident in my grip on the battle axe.

We finally reached the end of all those stairs.

And that end was a door.

A locked door, apparently. Because it had a latch, but didn't yield when Qala tried it.

She put away her sword then. Pulled a few tools from her pouch, crouched, and toyed with the lock by the light of Duron's flame until the lock clicked softly.

She moved a couple of stairs down, sword in one hand, dagger in the other. The rest of us readied our weapons.

Well, Duron raised his hands, but I was coming to think of them as his weapons. Not that I'd seen him fight yet...

Ig advanced to the top step. I'd figured he'd set a weapon aside, but he didn't. Used the head of his warhammer to turn the latch, and shoved at the door.

Which appeared to open outward.

Ig swore softly, then used the spike on the back of his hammer to turn the latch and pull open the door, his battle axe raised and ready.

Looked like a room, but I couldn't see any details from where I was, back down about a half-dozen stairs. Apart from a look at a ceiling that just looked like more rock. Same as we'd been walking under, only maybe wider and longer.

"I'd say we're here," Ig said, voice low and tense, but not urgent. Like he felt under threat, but not like he had to fight immediately.

I didn't know how to interpret his words, and tension unsettled the spiced dried meat in my belly.

"Slow and steady now," Qala said to all of us.

Edan turned to me. "Do not step beyond where we do, unless told to first."

I nodded.

We proceeded into the room. Ig and Qala first, then Duron and Edan, with me hanging back in the doorway.

It was a crypt.

The room stretched away from us like a rectangle, maybe ten strides across, and fifteen long. Along each long side, a row of marble columns. Seven each side. White veined with gold on the left side, black veined with silver on the right.

Down at the end of the room, a small dais with a wooden throne. On the throne, sat a mummified corpse, clad in the simple gray robes of a priest of Urtrens, complete with the right arm covered down to the hand and fingers, while the left arm was bare from the shoulder down, showing the tattoos of that priest's accomplishments in life.

Strangely, there weren't many...

Seating the mummified corpse of a priest in a crypt was a common enough practice, though not usually involving a chair that looked so much like a throne. An area where Urtrens was revered couldn't have its own local crypt until a priest died. Then an appropriate crypt was sanctified, and that priest was mummified to stand watch over the spirits of those who were buried within.

In this case, the watcher had only one spirit to watch over. Whoever lay in the single, raised tomb in the center of the room.

The tomb was carved from gray shades of rock I'd thought was granite, but might've been that bachite Ig had spoken of earlier. On the top was a bas-relief of a human figure, arms crossed over his chest, right over left.

Without thinking, I spat at the anathema.

"What's your problem?" Duron asked gruffly.

"The dead should be buried with the right hand beneath them and the left hand over the chest or eyes. Every priest of Urtrens would say so. But to bury someone – or represent a deceased individual – with their arms *crossed* on their chest, *especially* right over left, was to indicate a cross between the path of the righteous and the path of the blasphemer. A person like that was the worst of all – one who pretended to righteousness to lead the faithful astray."

"One reason I never went in much for religion," Ig said. "Too many rules."

"Well," Duron said, "meaning no offense here, Zian, that sounds about right for my great uncle. He was the sort who questioned everything, especially what he wasn't supposed to. And he'd join a group just to find out what it was hiding behind its rules."

I shook my head. "Not me he offended."

"Peace between you," Edan said. "The dead are the dead, and they did in life what they did in life. Nothing we say or do now will change that."

Duron narrowed his eyes at me, but I gave a sharp nod. He hesitated only a moment before giving me a nod back.

"You have come to the wrong place," a hollow voice said. "Turn and go back. You are not welcome here."

I realized with a start that it was the *watcher* who'd spoken. The mummified corpse was looking up at us through wizened eyes that were quite open.

"I am Duron," our wizard said, stepping forward. "I am of the blood of Egrun, and I have come to retrieve what he hid for the first worthy to claim it."

"I know the taste of the blood of Egrun," the watcher said. "Offer me a taste of your blood, that I may compare."

I stepped forward, raising my axe. "That is not a request Urtrens would bless."

"You know little of the deeper mysteries, my child."

"Then bless me, holy one," I said. "Bless me, that I shall see the difference between righteousness and blasphemy when the path before me lies shrouded in mist."

"Too many rules," Ig grumbled.

The watcher raised his left hand. Opened his mouth.

Nothing came out.

"It's a trap!" I shouted. "This is no true watcher!"

"I was no priest in life," the watcher's hollow voice scoffed. "Nor am I your 'watcher' in death. But I am guardian here. And I will taste the blood of this one who claims kinship with my charge."

"Everything else your uncle has done has been half a trick," Edan said, no intonation in their voice even now. "This may be a trick as well."

"The test is not for you, half-blood," the guardian said. "Your kind should've been exterminated centuries ago. Approach me and I shall bring them one step closer to their proper state."

"Sadly," Duron said softly, "that is consistent with what I know of Great Uncle Egrun's view of your people. A view I do not share, my friend."

Edan merely nodded.

Louder, Duron said, "I think I have to do this."

"I'll just come along then, shall I," Ig said, but not like it was a question. More like he was angry about something.

"Approach and your kind will move closer to extinction as well," the guardian said. "You are no more favored here than the half-blood."

"What of me?" Qala asked. "And this one?" She clapped me on the shoulder.

"You I do not trust to approach. And the other is not worth my attention." The guardian stood. "The petitioner alone, or leave this place."

Duron drew a deep breath, and slowly walked forward.

PART OF ME COULDN'T BELIEVE WHAT WAS HAPPENING.

This morning, the scariest thing I thought we might face was a crazed mountain cat.

Instead, we'd already fought that tentacled thing – a kaldip, they'd called it – and now, in my presence, a *dead man* stood. Talked. Made demands and issued threats.

But the strangest part was, I wasn't petrified with fear. If anything, I was angry at the blasphemies it spoke. And even though I'd never fought with a weapon before facing the kaldip, my arms itched to sink my battle axe into this ... *thing* that wore the pretense of priestly garb, but was nothing like a holy watcher over the spirits of the dead.

Nothing I could do, though, since Duron seemed set on going through with giving this thing a taste of his blood. A taste it claimed it could compare with that of his ancestor.

I didn't believe that for a moment. This thing had presented a false front right up until I'd challenged it to pronounce a holy blessing. Only then did it falter and change its story.

So while Duron slowly crossed the crypt, I tried to watch everywhere at once. The white marble columns to my left, the black marble columns to my right...

Wait.

The guardian, he sat *facing* me. And the tomb, the depicted body would have been facing me if it sat up.

Which meant that the gold-veined white marble columns were on their *right* and the silver-veined black marble ones on their *left*.

This whole crypt was an inversion of the ways of Urtrens the Holy.

I knew there were said to be neutral spirits in the world. Spirits that – by their nature – were somehow apart from the paths of righteousness and blasphemy.

But this place was designed to be dedicated to evil. Which meant that this guardian had to be worse than neutral.

It had to be unholy.

"Duron!" I shouted. "Don't do it! That thing's unholy! Has to be!"

My voice was urgent enough that the others all raised weapons. But Duron wouldn't heed my warning. He merely waved it away and kept walking.

He pulled a knife and raised one hand. Ready to cut himself and bleed for this foul thing.

It didn't wait. It grabbed him in an embrace and sank its teeth into his neck.

Duron howled in pain.

Qala and I both started forward, but Edan, "Wait. This might be its test."

But the thing showed no signs of stopping. And Duron's magic fire went out, leaving us in darkness.

The darkness lasted only a moment. Someone must've had a small pot of stickyfire, because I heard the sound of ceramics breaking and then the crypt was cast into the dim light and dancing shadows of a sweep of stickyfire on the ceiling.

Ig and Qala charged the guardian. I was about to join them, but panels opened on four of the pillars – two on each side – and sword-wielding...

Those were...

Those were skeletons of fallen warriors. Bereft of armor and shield now, they advanced on us with only their swords. But those swords looked more than deadly enough.

"Zian!" Edan shouted—

Well, really, that's not quite right. 'Shouting,' to me, implies urgency. And their tone was affectless as ever. So I guess it's more accurate to say Edan spoke loudly.

"Zian. Up onto the tomb with me."

Edan made it up there in a single jump. I needed to use one hand to boost myself up, but made it well before those skeletons got to us. They weren't moving all that fast.

Only two were headed for us anyway, one from each side. The other two were heading for the dais.

"Take these two," Edan said. "I'll aid our compatriots."

Could the dead be killed? Or ... stopped, I guess?

No time like the present to find out—

Wait.

I was wearing chain mail that only came about halfway down my thighs, and I'd just put myself in a position that made my enemies' easiest target my legs.

I jumped back down on the side facing the black columns. Unholy though this place might be, I came in from the holy direction, and I would fight from right to left as Urtrens would want me to.

Honestly, I didn't think that much about Urtrens on a daily basis. But in a place like this, how could I do otherwise?

The skeleton's jaw parted, maybe in some kind of soundless war cry. It raised its sword. But the haft of my axe was longer than that blade...

I set my feet and swung hard, right to left, twisting my hip into the blow as I would if I were cutting into a tree. Except I swung level, not slightly down.

I lopped off the skeleton's sword hand at the wrist. That was the good part.

The bad part, though, was that I'd swung too hard. Overbalanced.

Still. I was armed and the skeleton wasn't. I tried to use that. Spun with the strike. Hoping to use my momentum for my next blow.

Spun too slow.

The skeleton leaped on me. Its one hand clutching my armor. Its blunted arm pummeling at my forearms. Its teeth trying to reach my throat past my chain mail.

That was it for my balance. Fell to the hard stone floor. Dropped my axe. The skeleton started beating my chest with its arm, still worrying away at my coif with its teeth.

I could see its fellow getting closer. Looking eager in a way I couldn't explain.

But strong as that skeleton was, I had the weight of muscle and sinew to me and it had only bone.

I grabbed it by the shoulders and yanked it hard in the holy direction. I rolled on top. Punched it. Not that my punch did anything but hurt my hand.

Worse, in my haste, I hadn't accounted for the other skeleton.

Its sword came down at me.

No time to duck. No time to roll. No time to do anything at all.

That blow struck my head.

Pain lanced through me.

Darkness followed.

I half-expected to awaken to find myself standing before Taesark the Just, at the entrance to the Fields of Narath-Te. All wounds healed, but judgment pending.

Instead I awoke with a headache that felt like someone was trying to split my skull into logs for their hearth. I felt shaky and cold. When my eyes finally managed to flutter open, even the stickyfire on the crypt ceiling was bright enough to make me wince.

By the light of that stickyfire, I found myself looking up into the expressionless nut brown eyes of Edan.

"Do not move yet," Edan said softly. They brought a waterskin to my mouth. "Sip slowly. Work the water around your mouth before swallowing."

Suddenly I realized how parched I was. I didn't want to stop at a sip, but Edan pulled the skin away from me.

The feel of that water going down my sore throat, though, was glorious.

Why was my throat sore?

Edan held up three fingers. "How many?"

I swallowed. "Three."

"Does the room spin?"

I started to shake my head, but that made it hurt worse so I stopped with another wince. "No."

"Do you need to regurgitate?"

Regugi— oh. Vomit. "No. Stomach's a little queasy, but no."

"Lie still then while the other finish. I will tend you."

"Thank you," I said, easing my head back and realizing two things, and their obvious connection: my head lay on something soft, and Edan no longer had a cloak.

No sounds of combat, but I could hear hushed conversation and some scraping sounds over near the dais.

"What happened?" I asked.

"A skeleton caught you a heavy blow to the head with its sword. Knocked you unconscious. Fortunately, I had already dispatched its compatriots, and dealt with your two skeletons before they could finish you off."

"Thank you."

Edan nodded simply, and I got the impression that they didn't consider it worthy of thanks. Simply the appropriate thing to do at the time.

"How?" I asked. "I mean, arrows—"

"Arrows shot from my bow are more than capable of shattering a skull at short range. That was sufficient to rid the skeletons of their animating force."

"Should I have ... should I have swung for the skull?"

"With a weapon like your battle axe, you have options. Destroy or sever the skull. Destroy the ribs to get to the spine and sever that. Either way will work." Edan nodded. "You did well to sever the sword hand. Next time keep in mind that, unlike a human, such a blow will not even cause such a creature to slow. Let alone render it incapable of fighting."

I lay there for a moment. "You think there'll be a next time?"

"No matter what course you set yourself in life, you cannot eliminate that possibility. Though some choices will make it more likely than others."

"Well," I said, "obviously I'm not cut out for *this* life."

"What makes you say so?"

"I would have died twice down here, if not for you guys."

"Do you imagine yourself venturing into such places alone?"

I frowned. "Alone? Of course not."

"Any one of us could have died down here, without the others. One of us might have fallen to the kaldip, had you not found the courage to strike the blow that made it vulnerable again."

Edan patted my shoulder. "You contributed far more to this venture than any expected. Do not underrate yourself. Do you wish more water?"

"Please."

After giving me another sip, Edan said, "You did make one mistake, however, that you should learn from."

I didn't need to say the words, just look the question at them.

"You abandoned the advantage of high ground."

"But ... my unarmored legs..."

"You have not yet learned how to best use that position. I understand that. You will. But in abandoning the high ground, you expanded their options and made yourself more vulnerable."

I frowned. My head hurt too much to make much sense of what they were saying.

Edan patted my shoulder again. "Rest now. We will discuss tactics later."

I'm not sure how long I lay there, while Edan kept watch over me. I do know that I was more comfortable with Edan now than I'd expected to be. I thought I was even beginning to detect small, subtle changes in their intonations and facial expressions that suggested that maybe they weren't as affectless as I'd thought. Just ... subtle.

Eventually, though, the others rejoined us.

To my surprise, Duron didn't look hurt at all. I couldn't even see where the guardian had bitten him.

The guardian...

"That thing's dead?"

"Yes, yes," Ig said, but he was smiling. "The fell, unholy creature has been restored to its properly dead state. May it rest in pieces."

"Don't you mean—"

Ig's smile widened a little.

"Oh."

"Ig's a firm believer in dismembering such creatures," Qala said. She looked me over, but this time as though making sure I was all right, rather than the, well, other ways she'd been looking me over to that point.

"Ever gotten back to camp and found a severed hand crawling up your pant leg?" Ig said. "Because I have."

I frowned. "But dismembering wouldn't—"

"Does if you smash the hands," Ig said, hefting his warhammer.

Edan helped me to my feet and reclaimed their cloak.

Looking around now, I could see that the throne had been turned onto its side, and the tomb had been opened.

Anywhere else, that might've felt like defiling the dead. But this place was already unholy, so I figured there was nothing to defile.

"Did you find what you were looking for?" I asked.

"Oh, yes," Duron said, holding up an old, cracked leather tome. Gods help me, the man was actually grinning.

"There was also some gold, and a few gemstones," Qala said. "We'll divvy those up back in town."

"Plus, we'll see to your cut of the value of that book," Ig said, "or Kue Rinton'll never let us in the door again."

Ig said that like there was something more to say there. But he didn't say it. Instead, he nodded at Qala, who smiled at me.

"There *is* another option here," she said, stepping a little closer. "Duron found a map tucked inside that book he's clutching. Looks to indicate the true location of Drakkan Tor."

Drakkan Tor. Even I'd heard of Drakkan Tor. Said to have been the height of civilization some ... fifteen centuries ago. Magic and riches and beauty beyond anything known today. But accounts differed about where it lay...

"Fake?" I said.

"Likely real," Duron said, still grinning. "I've made a study of Drakkan Tor for decades, partially because of the family rumors that Great Uncle Egrun had found it. I've compared as many sources as I could find, and eliminated—"

"What he's trying to say," Qala said, rolling her eyes, "is that we have reason to think it might be legitimate. Enough reason that we're heading there next."

"After a day or two back in town," Ig insisted. "Spend a little of our newfound funds. Stock up on supplies."

"Drink too much ale," Edan said, and now I could hear it. The slightest change in intonation that sounded...

That was a joke! Edan had made a joke! And I'd caught it!

I chuckled *along with everyone else.*

"So what do you say, handsome?" Qala said, quirking her smile a little more. "We can pay you off and let you get back to ... whatever it is you do for Kue Rinton. *Or* ... we can give you a full share of what we found here, and you can come with us to Drakkan Tor."

"I—"

"Do not decide now," Edan said. "You have suffered a blow to the head, and doubtless your desire for Qala will influence you. You need only decide before we leave."

I nodded. Tentatively, since my head still hurt quite a bit.

WE LEFT THE ... TUNNELS? CATACOMBS? I WASN'T SURE WHAT THE right word was. Point is, we left them just as cautiously as we'd entered them.

Well, *almost* as cautiously. Qala didn't need to check every step of where we'd already been. But I was pretty sure the others still considered the possibility of us having to fight again at least once between the crypt and that first, dusty corridor.

No fight came, though. And we got back to the horses to find them impatient for food, water, and exercise, but otherwise pretty much fine.

It was nighttime when we emerged from those doors into the "cave" beneath were that waterfall used to be.

No one lay in wait for us, which I found encouraging. The others weren't surprised though.

The twin moons were high, and full enough that we could see reasonably well, which meant it was close to midnight.

Edan and Qala insisted on checking the ground inside that indentation before we left, and found tracks that apparently proved that about a dozen someones had come looking for the source of my sneeze.

That changed the way we left. Instead of mounting and riding away, we walked the horses through the chasm as quietly as we could, then mounted up and rode out into the foothills and back to that clearing where we'd first spent the night.

It's funny. While we'd been down in those tunnels, I hadn't thought of the air as stuffy or anything. I mean, yeah, that first corridor was dusty beyond anything I'd previously imagined. And when that awful fetid smell of that kaldip had been worse still. But in general, down there, it hadn't seemed so bad.

But once we got to that clearing in the light of the twin moons, and I had a chance to stop and relax, I found a whole new level of appreciation for the smell of the clean spring air and nut elm trees.

The moonlight looked different too. Crisper. Cleaner. And the dirt—

"It's not the tunnels," Qala said, smiling at me from her bedroll. She was sitting cross-legged. I'd always thought of that position as a little awkward, but she made it look graceful.

"What's not?" I asked.

She chuckled, and so did Ig.

"World looks a little more inviting, doesn't it." Qala didn't make it a question. "Air's a little sweeter. The moonlight's a little prettier. Bet that dried, spiced meat even tastes better."

I smiled. She was right. The spices of the dried meat I'd been gnawing on *did* taste better.

"You had your first brush with death," Ig said. "Makes every reminder that your alive a little more … vivid. In fact…"

He turned a broad, knowing smile on Qala.

"I wish," she said, matching his smile. "But not here in front of you lot. It can wait until we have a proper room and a proper bed."

My pulse quickened at her implications, and I suddenly found myself wishing we were back in the Purple Gryphon right that moment.

Qala must've seen it in my eyes. She winked at me. "Soon enough, handsome. And trust me, it'll be worth the wait."

With a thought like *that* in my head, no way I could sleep anytime soon. So I shared the first watch with Ig, while he quietly explained what to look and listen for. How to position myself. When and why to move around, and when to remain still.

It was all more involved than I'd expected. And by the time our watch was over, I was more than ready to get some rest.

Edan took the second watch. There wasn't really time for a third.

We rose with the dawn in the morning, and didn't bother with breakfast. We broke camp, mounted up, and rode back across the valley to the Purple Gryphon.

We made good time under the blaze of a heat wave that was going strong. Wasn't much past midday when we were dismounting outside Kue Rinton's stables and gathering our gear to bring inside.

And apparently I'd learned Edan's riding tips pretty well. Because I can't say that a half-day's ride had been *fun*, I wasn't nearly as sore getting back as I'd been going out. Which had me feeling good as I approached the stables, leading Dandelion.

It was Poli who took Dandelion's reins from me, trying to murder me with his gaze while he did.

Funny thing there. Two days ago, I would have squirmed under the intensity of his glare. Maybe said something inoffensive or reassuring. Maybe just tried to slink away.

But I just couldn't bring myself to worry about Poli and his gaze. Whatever problems he and Laren had, they didn't involve me. Whether he believed that or not.

So I didn't squirm, but I didn't smile either. I just looked right past him and went inside with the others.

The kitchen was busy, and overflowing with the wonderful savory scents of Beka's lamb stew, along with baking rye bread, and some kind of sweet cinnamon pastry. All of the kitchen hands were busy, but as the group of us crossed the kitchen, heading for the main room, Laren stopped beating her bread dough and gazed up at me, lips parted in what I thought was surprise.

There was a *lot* going on in Laren's eyes as she looked at me. More than I could begin to parse. But honestly, I couldn't bring myself to worry about that either. So I just gave her a smile and a nod and kept moving.

Our lunch was waiting, and I was more than ready for it.

The main room in the Purple Gryphon was already in full swing. Two-thirds full of patrons eating and drinking and talking and laughing. Somehow cutting through the dull roar of the patrons, a fiddler played a quick, jaunty tune while a good dozen patrons thumped the time on bench tables.

"Perhaps we should see about a private room for lunch," Edan said.

"No!" Ig answered, looking shocked. "This is *just* what we need! I'll grab us some space."

He started off into the crowd.

"And I'll keep him from starting any fights," Qala said, squeezing my arm and hurrying after him.

Duron frowned after them. "Better if we catch up to them now."

"I agree," Edan said, leading the way through the crowed to the seats Ig had just managed to clear – apparently without violence, though possibly with the threat of violence, I couldn't be sure – well away from the hearth and the fiddler, where we would have stone wall to one side.

Drianna was working the tables on this shift, and no sooner did the five of us have our seats than she brought us a round of ale and promised food to follow quickly.

"Better bring extra ale for Ig," I said with a smile.

IT'S FUNNY. I'D ALWAYS GOTTEN ALONG WELL WITH EVERYONE AT THE Purple Gryphon – Poli excepted, of course – but I don't think I'd ever felt as comfortable sharing a meal with any of them as I felt during that lunch with Ig, Qala, Duron and Edan.

Maybe it was what Qala had been saying about facing death for the first time. I'd heard passing soldiers and mercenaries talk about the camaraderie created by facing battle together, and what the five of us had done wasn't all that different.

But through that lunch of wonderful lamb stew and rye bread, I felt relaxed and happy. Comfortable enough to make jokes, not just laugh at others' jokes. And that was a new experience for me.

As we finished up, Qala leaned closer and whispered in my ear, "I need a bath. Care to join me?"

"Oh, yes," I said, and got as far as standing before Drianna stepped up to us.

"Zian," she said, sounding nervous, "I'm supposed to tell you the boss wants a word."

"I'll take care of your gear," Edan said. "Kue Rinton should not be kept waiting."

Qala huffed out an irritated breath, but gave my arm a squeeze. "Don't make me wait too long, handsome, or I'll start that bath without you."

When I knocked on the door of Kue Rinton's office behind the bar, it opened.

No one turned the handle, and no one was standing in the doorway, but it opened.

Kue Rinton was already sitting behind her small, red wood desk. The table behind her had been cleared. Candles burned in their iron sconces along the river stones of the walls, but I realized now that there must've been another source of light.

Because the office was brighter than it should have been. Right up to the wooden catwalk up above, beyond which all was darkness.

I was just starting to wonder what was up there when the door closed behind me.

I looked around, saw no one, and when I looked back, Kue Rinton's eyes caught me.

Once more she looked right through me with those purple eyes of hers, and I shivered just as I always had. So maybe I hadn't really changed all that much. I don't know.

I forced myself to at least look elsewhere while she assessed me. She was wearing a dark green dress. Simple cut, with a high neckline and long sleeves. She wore her vivid black hair in a tail that came over her left shoulder and trailed down her torso.

"Good," Kue Rinton said with a ghost of a smile somewhere in those penetrating purple eyes. "You've come back alive and reasonably intact. Quite a blow to the head you suffered, though."

How she knew that, I couldn't guess. Unless she really was a witch. But even that idea didn't frighten me as it once would have.

"Nothing you won't recover fully from, with time," she said. "I presume that happened during a fight, and not because Dandelion threw you?"

"Dandelion wouldn't throw anybody," I said, then found myself telling her the whole story. The night in the hills. Entering the chasm. Finding the hidden door. My sneeze. Our rush in with the horses. The search. The second hidden door and the riddles we solved.

The kaldip. The guardian. The skeletons. Everything.

"Well," she said, when I finished. "They certainly expected more of you than simple guidance across the countryside, I'd say."

"They've offered to let me join them. They think... They think they've found a map that could lead to Drakkan Tor."

She nodded slowly. "I wouldn't say that outside this office. That name ... would draw attention you don't need."

"I'm not sure why I said it here, to be honest, ma'am."

"I think you know."

"You really are a witch?"

"Does that bother you?"

Huh. It didn't. I'd expected that my heart would've lurched or my face would've gotten hot or something, hearing her confirm that rumor.

But no...

"A few days ago, it would've," I said. "Not so much now, though."

She gave a slow, thoughtful nod. "And this invitation to join them. Do you intend to accept?"

"I'm supposed to sleep on it."

Kue Rinton raised an eyebrow at me. "And perhaps sate some of your hunger of Qala first?"

"Edan seemed to think I'd make a smarter decision if ... well..."

"Edan is quite right." She narrowed her eyes slightly. "Do you feel pressured to accept this?"

"No, ma'am."

"Good. Realize that if you go with them, you are in for long stretches of travel. Of sleeping on hard and sometimes rocky ground. Of eating only what you can carry or hunt. Along with moments of stark terror, any of which might bring your days to an untimely end."

"But that's not all, ma'am. There's wonder, too. And magic. And secrets. And going places that no one's—"

"—been in hundreds of years, maybe more," Kue Rinton said. "Yes. That's all true too." She gave me a searching look I felt down to my bones. "But that's not all, is it? You've already formed a thread of the connection that binds them like family."

I nodded.

"You've already decided. Haven't you."

I nodded. "Nothing looks the same to me now, ma'am. I think … I think maybe this was what I was hoping for the first day I walked in here."

"Yes," she said with a sigh. "I think that's true." She cocked her head slightly. "What about Yinda?"

"I'll miss her, ma'am. But she and I have been going separate ways for years now."

Kue Rinton nodded, as though considering what else she might say.

"If there's nothing more for now, ma'am, may I be excused?"

"Oh? Something pressing?" She smiled slightly. "Ah. Of course. Qala."

I smiled.

"She's a better choice for you than Laren anyway."

"Laren, ma'am? I've never—"

"Oh, I know you haven't. And maybe it's better that you leave, and take that temptation away from her."

I didn't know how to answer that.

"Know that you'll always be welcome here, Zian," she said. "Whatever the circumstances of your return. Whether you need only a room for the night, a job, or assistance, you will always find it at the Purple Gryphon."

"Thank you, ma'am," I said, touched.

"On your way then, with my blessing. And take care."

"You too, ma'am," I said with a smile. My heart soared. I was really going to do this!

I stepped out of her office then, and into my new life. As an adventurer.

SIGN UP FOR STEFON'S NEWSLETTER

Stefon loves to keep in touch with his readers, and loves to keep you reading. The best way for him to do both is for you to sign up for his newsletter.

Sign up at http://www.stefonmears.com/join

If you sign up for Stefon's newsletter, you get...

- Monthly updates about his publishing and travel schedules
- His latest news, in brief, and answers to reader questions
- A free short story for signing up
- List-only offers and occasional specials
- Plus a free short story every month!

ABOUT THE AUTHOR

Stefon Mears loves a good fantasy inn or tavern. Stefon has more than thirty novels to his credit, and he never stops writing. He earned his M.F.A. in Creative Writing from N.I.L.A., and his B.A. in Religious Studies (double emphasis in Ritual and Mythology) from U.C. Berkeley. He's a lifelong gamer and fantasy fan. Stefon lives in Portland, Oregon, with his wife and three cats.

Look for Stefon online:
www.stefonmears.com
himself@stefonmears.com